The Mountains May Depart

by Ryan Rickrode

Unsolicited Press
Portland, Oregon
www.unsolicitedpress.com
info@unsolicitedpress.com
619–354–8005

THE MOUNTAINS MAY DEPART
Copyright © 2026 Ryan Rickrode
All Rights Reserved.
Printed in the United States of America.
First Edition.
ISBN: 978-1-963115-80-2

This is a work of fiction. Any resemblance to actual persons, living or dead, or to actual events is purely coincidental. No part of this publication may be reproduced, stored in a retrieval system, transmitted, or distributed in any form or by any means—electronic, mechanical, photocopying, recording, or otherwise—without the prior written permission of the publisher.

Distributed by Asterism Books
https://asterismbooks.com/

For wholesale orders:
Asterism Books
568 1st Avenue South, Ste 120
Seattle, WA 98104
(206) 485-4829
info@asterismbooks.com

Cover Design: Kathryn Gerhardt
Editor: Summer Stewart

Praise for THE MOUNTAINS MAY DEPART

"This is a beautiful book. Short, sweet, tough, brave, tender, resilient, heartbreaking, true. All that. Ryan Rickrode has written a terse and beguiling and remarkably beautiful novel. Read this."

—**Bret Lott**, bestselling author of *Jewel,* an Oprah's Book Club selection

"Throughout this novella, Ryan Rickrode not only masterfully interweaves both points-of-view as a husband and wife consider fleeing from a marriage wounded by tragedy, but also uses that struggle to explore the fundamental search for life's meaning and purpose, a universality that should engage a wide variety of readers."

—**Gary Fincke**, author of *The Out-of-Sorts: New and Selected Stories*

"In *The Mountains May Depart*...Ryan Rickrode evocatively and lyrically reveals the nuances of how this couple navigates a new world they hadn't anticipated and how their actions and their views of each other powerfully affect their future."

—**Nathaniel Lee Hansen**, freelance editor and former editor-in-chief of *The Windhover*

"Grief isolates Rickrode's characters; it is the fulcrum upon which their agony seesaws. Should they fight or flee? Forgive or forget? Rickrode walks a daunting tightrope between tension and disclosure. The juxtaposition of what is thought versus what is said when two people are poisoned with resentment is maddeningly authentic and forces us to examine how we resist choosing love in our own lives. This book is a small whirlwind!"

—**Tara Stillions Whitehead**, author of *The Year of the Monster*

to my wife, to my parents,
and to my son,
with love and gratitude

Forgive and forget, they say, but that is surely wrong. . . . Love does not say to the beloved that it does not matter. Spare me the sentimental love that tells me who I am and what I do does not matter.

— Richard John Neuhaus,
Death On A Friday Afternoon

i. matins, compline

The sun climbs the mountain, the morning light skulks in. She wakes to the sound of her husband waking, and she lies still.

He moves and she listens. The shush of his drawers, his trek to the bathroom. A scrape of stubble as he kisses her on the cheek, the weight of his feet on the stairs. The coffee begins to percolate. The back door thumps shut. He is gone.

When she's more asleep than awake she can almost recall the old pleasures of near-dawn: her husband's small noises mingling with that hot-coffee smell, the cotton sheets tangled in the sunshine, the slow fill of the house, a deep breath before the exhale of day. But it isn't before, and rather than wait for things that won't come, she forces herself out of bed and onto her knees. She does this every morning while he jogs. It brings her no comfort. She does not feel close to God when she prays.

She prays anyway. She prays, "Incline your ear, O Lord, and answer me, for I am poor and needy." She prays, "Bless the Lord, O my soul, and forget not all his benefits—who forgives you all your iniquity, who heals all your diseases, who redeems your life from the Pit."

In her prayers God is like an unseen animal, immense and aloof, stamping and snorting in the fog, and she is taken by the audacity of the psalms, so many imperative sentences: "Hide your face from my sins," "Do not cast me from your presence," "Restore to me the joy of your salvation." As if God will do these things simply because she tells him to. There is as much sense in praying the psalms as there is in asking the Bitterroots to cast themselves into the Pacific. Who is she?

The words come like pointed fingers, what she is, and she tries not to think of them, not yet. She reads the sentences on the page, forming them with her lips and speaking them aloud. She tries hard to mean them. It's like attempting to start a fire with two sticks: "For God alone my soul in silence waits, from Him comes my salvation."

She closes the prayerbook when she hears him return. He thumps through the back door into the kitchen, vigorously noisy in the way only a man can be, taking a cup from the cupboard, filling it with ice, filling it with water, glugging it down.

As he sacks the kitchen she dresses for the day, black slacks, green polo. When she hears him heading upstairs she takes a final look in the mirror, her unwashed hair.

She meets him in the hallway, red-faced, still perspiring.

"Good morning," he says.

"Good morning."

Every morning she feels more certain she should leave him, that leaving would be the loving action. Kissing Dan is like saying the psalms, outrageous winter faith.

In the kitchen she spreads the newspaper across the table. The internet is too alive, too crowded. She's stopped logging in. Instead she scans the pages of *The Missoulian* as she sips at her coffee.

She is trying to teach herself to take it black, has found the sugar easy to part with but misses the cream. Some days she'll retrieve the half-and-half from the fridge and feel a tug of guilt as she's stirring it in, but today she takes it black. She flips through the paper, skimming headlines on her way to the comics: something about the president, something about the Vatican, a meth lab busted in Butte, the Top Hat Bar is closing and reopening under new ownership.

Never before has she had so much time to read—no papers to grade, no e-mails to delete, no (no, don't think of those things)—but so little appetite for books. At Christmas she picked up an Alice Munro collection only to put it down halfway through the first story. All she can manage is the newspaper and occasionally, when she needs to remind herself that she is still, somehow, a poet, a little T.S. Eliot, gloomy and cerebral, a distraction. Beyond that literature just asks for too much: empathy, emotion, imaginative energy, *Come, follow me,* but she just can't. The fictional sorrows of Munro's women are too much. She is sticking with Dagwood and Garfield and J. Alfred Prufrock until it's time to leave for the laundromat, and Dan is already jaunting down the stairs.

"How's Ziggy?"

"The pharmacist shot him in the face with one of those trick flowers full of water, because 'laughter is the best medicine.'"

"That's funny," he says without laughing. These days he's always speaking loudly. It's as if he's confused being sad with being hearing impaired. He is thirty and she is thirty-one. Married seven years, and it feels like longer. It feels like forever. Maybe now that he's asked about Ziggy he'll be quiet.

Through the winter he was acceptably sullen, but now with spring tilting into summer he's grown manic, jolly one moment and brooding the next. Good God, the summer—May's nearly here and Dan is done teaching the first week of June. What will she do when school lets out and he's just . . . around? He insists on dashing himself on her sadness. He ferrets her out, finds her crying in the bedroom, the office, the pantry. "What's the matter?" *What a stupid question.* She says, "That's a stupid question." But he keeps trying. It can't go on forever. He sits down with his cereal bowl, and though he makes no further attempts at conversation she can feel him searching her face for signs as she reads the Dear Abby: "Dishwasher Sows Discord Between Husband and Wife." He stares quite openly. It's as if she's the dregs of a tea cup or the entrails of a bird.

His spoon scrapes the bottom of the bowl and he carries it to the sink, and she is glad, if reflexively annoyed, when he jingles the keys like a leash. "Ready to go?"

She nods. To the garage, to the car. The sun is peering over the mountains, they drive across the bridge. The sky is stretched with rays of thin white light. All this was once underwater, a glacial lake, the whole valley.

When he pulls into the parking lot of the laundromat he leans across the armrest for a hug.

"I love you," he says.

She speaks the response. She tries to mean it: "I love you too."

A dead thing within him has wormed itself awake. Two months and a year since Sam died and Dan has begun to catch himself catching glimpses of Carolyn Lakes.

Sam was his son. —*is my son. Sam was and* is *my son.* The boy was four years old when he went. That was last February, but suddenly somehow it is April again. It is April and the world is warming and Carolyn Lakes' knees are peering out from beneath the hemline of her skirt as she flips through an old issue of *NEA Today* on the far side of the teachers' lounge. She's blond, two years out of college, five or six years his younger. She dresses professional, but underneath . . .

He hates that he has these thoughts, but there they are and lately he is inclined to indulge them. A part of him keeps saying that he deserves these glimpses, that it is April and the world is warming and he deserves restitution.

In the mornings, every morning, as he puts on his running shoes, he resolves to swallow back his if-onlys: if only Sarah hadn't been fumbling with her cellphone, if only she hadn't been in such a rush, if only she'd checked her blind spot before merging, then—

It's all as neat as ninth grade geometry, but he will swallow back these if-onlys forever if he has to, because he loves his wife *goddammit* and she blames herself too much already. He is thirty, almost thirty-one, and he knows how the story goes: *Couple loses son, only son. Couple falls apart.* At night he can feel the narrative passing over their house like weather, and there are moments when he is seized with a desire to hold her and hold her, his wife, his best friend. The brisk way she undresses in the evening, a toss of her hair, lately it takes almost nothing, but in the bedroom she shudders at his touch.

He rolls over, big spoon, and kisses the nape of her neck. Wisps of her hair now cling to his beard.

She says, "I'm too tired for cuddling."

"You're tense," he says, and with the pad of his thumb he begins to work a small circle into the muscles of her shoulder. She allows him the massage but takes no pleasure from it (no little moans). He soon stops.

"I love you," he says.

"I love you too."

"Good night."

"Good night, Dan."

Outside, in the night, there is a rumble like thunder as a length of train cars comes slamming to a stop. He begins to count to himself. He counts in multiples of thirteen—*twenty-six, thirty-nine, fifty-two, sixty-five. . . .*

Beside him her breaths swell and then deepen, and he is dimly jealous, though he knows she'll startle awake once or twice before the morning: she'll sit up and look around and when he asks what's the matter she'll say nothing. Nightmares, he suspects, or back pain from the crash. Maybe both.

He is tired of not knowing. That morning, after his shower, while Sarah was downstairs with the newspaper, he entered her office and opened her writer's notebook (a cardinal sin in their house). The latest entry was the scraps of a poem, not promising:

> *these are the days you would summarize and skip over*
> *if only you knew there was some sentence coming after*

A line break, perhaps a pause, then she wrote:

> *these days which we would cross out*
> *God takes note of them I suppose*
> *I suppose he allows us to suffer*
> *so that he might wring out of us something true:*
>
> *Lord, I have loved you,*
> *but only for my own sake.*

Lord my ass, he thought, and shut the book.

Before the accident they were religious people, regulars at a church that was also a coffeeshop, a hip little place with Mumford & Sons lyrics stenciled on the walls. At night in bed they used to join hands and thank God for the day and remember the less fortunate, and it hadn't felt foolish, not then.

What she thinks of God now he doesn't know. She's gone in for high liturgy, Lutheranism, a white-hair-and-hearing-aides crowd that takes its communion every Sunday. She seems to find some solace in the rituals. *Now we stand. Now we sit.* It's a fortress of a church, more German than Montanan. Every time he follows her up the stones steps to the building, he imagines arrows fired from the stained-glass slits of the windows, hot pitch spilling down its sides.

When she closes her eyes for the Brief Order of Confession and Forgiveness, he pretends she is speaking not of God, but of him: *If we say we have no sin we deceive ourselves and the truth is not in us. But if we confess our sins* Dan *who is faithful and just will forgive our sins and cleanse us from all unrighteousness.*

He knows, or is sometimes certain that he knows, that inside she is as wracked as he is—although, hell, for all she lets on she may only be composing a grocery list behind those cold breakfast table eyes each morning. Her eyes are like the dark eyes of a bird, indecipherable, and if he can't decode her grief, how can he participate in it? *How can I if she won't let me?* he says, not to God, of course, but to himself and to the ceiling.

He is getting angry. *Deep breath.* The shadows in the bedroom are vague shapes cast by the street lights and the moon. They are far from their antecedents. Again he closes his eyes. *Two eighty-six . . . two ninety-nine, three twelve . . . .*

Two years ago he and Sarah were like two whirling cogs meshed together, velcroing shoes, cleaning spills, kissing cuts. Bath time, bed time. They'd made love while their son was asleep.

He was wondering then, in those days, whether she too might want another baby, a second Sam, a little sister or brother. It was logical. Was back then. It wasn't so long ago that she took the story book from his hands and corrected him with a whisper, a double message, the words warm and arousing in his ear. She said, "Blue Beard is neither a pirate nor a children's story," but her eyes flashed like doves in the rocks.

She slid into the other side of the narrow little bed, wedging Sam in between them. He was sleepy but not asleep, twisting in his jammies and pouting for the confiscated tale. Dan had promised him pirates and parrots and maps to buried treasure.

She stroked the boy's blond hair, still wispy just a little though he was a baby no longer. She said, "Can Mommy read you one of her favorites?"

Emotion moved like little red clouds across his smooth cheeks. Verging on tears he pressed his face into Sarah's side. Her fingers through his hair kept him quiet.

She read aloud: "'Attention please, we're going to begin. When we've got to the end we'll know more than we do now.'"

The cadence of the story was not naturally her own. It took a few sentences for Sarah to fall into it: a wicked troll had made a mirror, and that mirror marred everything it reflected, making beautiful landscapes look like boiled spinach and honest men look grotesque. Now the troll and his troll students were flying the mirror up to heaven to mock God and his angels (how she divined what was and wasn't "appropriate for children" was beyond him), "'and the higher they flew the more the glass grimaced till they could scarcely keep hold.'" The mirror shattered on the ground, slivers lodged in people's eyes, and those people then had only eyes for what was wrong with the world, and other slivers lodged in people's hearts "'and that was horrible, for each heart became just like a lump of wet ice,'" and Sarah's voice grew stronger as she came to the end of the section: "'The evil one laughed till he split, it tickled him so. Out in the world bits of glass were flying in the air. Now we are to hear all about it.'"

She turned the page to read on, then paused. "Sam-baby?"

A little whistle had settled into his nostrils.

She kissed his forehead and mouthed: *I think he's out.*

They slid cautiously off the bed.

In the hallway: "Should we call it a night?"

Again those dove-y eyes.

"I'm not so tired."

She took his hand and led him to their room.

Here they are, side by side but with air in between, like two parallel lines extending untouching into infinity. They used to sleep with their ankles intertwined, but now— No, the thing to picture is two parallel lines meeting at the horizon. An apex. He will get them there. She just needs more time, that's all.

In the meantime he will wash his mind with large numbers, multiply himself into slumber, and he won't think about— No, he won't think of *her* at all. He won't think about anything. Not a thing. Nothing.

Three seventy-seven . . . three ninety . . . four hundred and three . . .

. . . four sixteen . . . .

. . . four twenty-nine . . .

. . . four forty-two . . . .

. . . four fifty-five . . .

. . . four sixty-eight . . . .

ii. happiness so easily

He wakes at five and rolls softly out of bed so as not to wake Sarah. He puts on a pot of coffee, then takes a loose, easy pace out the back door. He alternates, jogging for six minutes and then walking for three, and in this way travels through the tunnel under the railroad tracks and past the downtown shops toward the river.

Around him the city is stirring with delivery trucks, dog walkers, bicyclists, and other joggers. Missoula, Montana: a city of beautiful dogs and athletic women, attractive women in the shops, on the sidewalks, at the Bark Park with their laughing canines. He's always known this about Missoula (is it the mountain air? is it the organic produce?) but not since his days as a student at the U of M has he felt so acutely aware of their beaming presence in the streets. He quickens his pace.

At the start of each run he works hard to enter a Zen-like state in which he is thinking and feeling nothing. He is combustion. He is motion. The numbness is key as the town is spectered with memories. They lie in wait, lurking outside the bus station and the bars, in the parking lot of the Albertson's, whole montages of them tapping lead pipes against open palms.

As summer retakes the valley and the snow withdraws up the slopes he can feel the memories growing restless, more aggressive. It has become difficult not to think of the old days as he runs, surrounded by the mountains, passing the old bars and cafes where he and Sarah first began to grow into each other. But thinking of the before only stirs up the after, and now he is bitterly recalling how he came home last night to the smell of spicy marinara on the stove but with Sarah nowhere in sight. He found her in the pantry, crying over a clear plastic barrel of animal-shaped crackers.

"Baby?"

He steps into the pantry to give her a hug. She pulls away.

"I'm fine."

Clearly you are not fine. But she's already smudged her makeup onto the shoulder of her sweater. She is stirring the sauce and asking him how was his day, the usual script, and he feels like punching drywall. But he swallows it back. He tells how his classes went. She summarizes her day at the laundromat. Dinner is forks squeaking on plates.

His watch gives a beep and he slows his pace to a brisk walk. He thought he'd gotten good at it, not thinking while he runs, but lately he keeps stumbling.

What he likes about the running, what drew him to it back in March, is the way it can consume him—there is time, there is distance, there is a manageable amount of pain. When his feet fall into a rhythm his brain thinks of these and nothing else. When will the endorphins kick in? Am I keeping a good pace?

On the best days he barely registers the things he passes as he passes them—the sun glinting off windows, the birds in the leafless winter bushes, a bicyclist with a baby trailer in tow, the mountains which say nothing—but today as he jogs past the James Bar with its alley door propped open he catches the scent of the fryers in the kitchen, an odd smell this early in the day, and he is jumped by the memories, struck across the knees and dumped into a trunk, transported back to the old days, the *old* old days before he knew Sarah, when the city was wholly new and full of wonders: glass bottles in the windows of the thrift stores catching sunlight, the word LOVE spelled out in rags woven into the chain-link fence by the highway, chunks of ice floating down the Clark Fork like souls.

He'd spent a year and a half studying statistics at a large mountainless school in Iowa before transferring to the University of Montana. He was a Montanan by birth, raised in Butte, and after a bout in the hospital with the flu he'd found himself wanting to be someplace more like home.

But Missoula—known round the state as the Hippie Mecca of Montana—was neither Ames nor Butte, but something else altogether: a city of fly fishermen, scruffy hipsters, backpackers, beautiful girls, beer brewers, professors, football fans, and people on bikes (so many bikes). There were dirty mandolinists on the street corners and baristas with master's degrees in the drive-through coffee huts, neighborhoods in town with doe grazing in the front yards and chickens cooped in the back. Sarah, who read good books, often told her family out east that a river *literally* runs through it. It was a city of five bridges with a university nestled against the mountains. There was a large L on the mountain to the left of the river for Loyola, the Catholic high school, and an M on the mountain to the right, just above the U of M campus. On the hills to the north was a peace sign.

What Dan liked most about the James Bar, besides their elk burgers and truffle fries, was the quote engraved on the concrete of its outer wall:

Myths and legends die hard in America. We love them for the extra dimension they provide, the illusion of near-infinite possibility to erase the narrow confines of most men's reality. Weird heroes and mould-breaking champions exist as living proof to those who need it that the tyranny of the rat race is not yet final.

He used to imagine himself filming a movie set in Missoula with its opening scene a long shot directly on this wall. After the audience had had enough time to read the words the hero would walk past the wall from left to right, and then the camera would cut to something else. What that shot would be he didn't know. He was a math major and had never been very good at thinking up stories, and that was what he needed: a plot he could thread through the city, a way of arranging his love for these mountains and these buildings into a narrative.

This is how he used to tell it: when Sarah sat down beside him in American History he knew, knew right then for certain, that she was the one. He asked if he could borrow a pen. They got to talking. She mentioned a Bible study she held in her dorm and he slyly asked if he could join (and here she would always interrupt: *That's not how it happened at all. I had to invite you six times. I all but seduced you for Jesus*).

He'd never been to a "Bible study" before, but it didn't strike him as a daunting thing to sit in on, certainly not when it was held in a pretty girl's dorm room, and he was already more or less a Christian at the time, baptized as an infant and brought to church by his parents on Sundays, and the idea of God made sense to him. It made sense when he sorted out polynomials and it made sense when he stood at the M on the mountain and looked out from the city to see the distant peaks that cupped the valley.

But if Dan was a Christian, Sarah was something else: a saint, a mystic, a wizard. She was a convert. Religion in her upper-middle-class family had been a taboo, as shushed as sex. She'd found God her freshman year through a Christian club on campus and was baptized in the frigid waters of the Clark Fork the spring of her sophomore year. By the time Dan met her, a year later when he was a sophomore and she was a junior, she seemed able to glimpse God everywhere, in the sun behind snowy clouds, in the ice on the river, in the smell of white chicken chili on the stove.

Each week Dan lingered a little longer in her room after the others went home, and she never seemed to mind. In fact, she seemed to like it. Though she was a year ahead of him in school they were both twenty-one, and on Tuesdays after Bible study they began venturing into the downtown bars that served good beer from local breweries, beers with names like Cold Smoke and Trout Slayer, and this did not feel like a contradiction to their Christian faith. On the contrary, it felt right, the proper and worshipful response to God's Missoula.

She chronicled God's appearances—"hierophanies" she called them—in a Moleskine notebook. She was a double major in English and religious studies and she could lead people through the Bible as if it were an ecosystem, a thick humid place where every word was breathing and interconnected. It was not the code of conduct he'd thought that it was. It was something deeper and more mysterious, a current that could grab you. *This line alludes to how God the Creator conquered the dark waters of chaos. These verses are a hymn the earliest Christians used to sing. "Israel" means "struggles with God."* For Sarah God was not distant—he spoke to her through strange timings, gut feelings, and odd words repeated in disparate contexts.

She sketched often in those days, the sun on the rocks in the river, the shadows of the clouds on the mountains, the sparrows in his weedy little yard. She'd grown up in a boxy suburb of Annapolis and was enthralled with the landscape of western Montana and could never quite capture the beating heart of it on the page. It was easier, she said, with words, but not the same, and she was relentless when it came to her poems, often x-ing out entire stanzas. She would write and rewrite until she no longer felt dissatisfied and was perhaps even pleased.

He kept Sarah's sketches and poems taped to the window in his bedroom, and he would read them in the morning before pulling his socks from his drawer. In "Negative Theology" she wrote: "What God is not / is not even the sound of birdsong / out the window on a cold day."

She said what she liked about him was his steadfastness, his calf muscles, and his red hair. (Here in the retelling she would always agree: *True, I'll give you that.*) That winter he took her cross-country skiing in the Rattlesnake and then hiking in Glacier when the weather turned warm. When they started to become serious about each other later that semester he took her to the hot springs in Idaho where he saw her in a bikini for the first time. At his drafty apartment she taught him how to caramelize onions, sear broccoli, sauté chicken, and afterwards they would make out on his roommate's couch with the smell of chopped garlic on their hands.

There seemed to be nothing she could do he didn't love, and it amazed him how easily they strung the sunsets and the mountains together into days of prayer and good beer. He'd never thought such rhythmic happiness could be possible—happiness, yes, but so easily?

They married the summer after he graduated, when she was a year into her master's degree. Too early said her parents, and his too, in a more roundabout way, but the happiness endured as he scraped them by on his substitute teacher's wages.

They found the strangest thing about being married was how easy it was to be naked together. The sex itself was clumsy—while dating they'd accepted (or, rather, she'd convinced him to accept) what their faith taught, that sex was for marriage, so neither of them really knew what they were doing—but they reminded each other often that they had all the time in the world to figure it out, to practice, and when they looked back on their decision to wait they felt good about it. He wondered if maybe it helped explain the strangeness, how they could be naked together without feeling naked.

In those early days they talked about it often, the oddness and delight of it. Neither of them had ever really loved their own bodies. Sarah was boney-pale and hated her scrawniness—she used make-up to hide the blue vein on her forehead—and Dan was the opposite, always doughy, at times even puffy. He'd never felt comfortable changing in locker rooms where people might see bits of him jiggle, but with Sarah it was different. When she looked at him in the bedroom when he was wearing nothing but tube socks she liked it, and it felt as easy as standing before her in jeans and a t-shirt. He was not embarrassed. They were naked and not ashamed.

Enough of that. He gives his cheeks one, two, three light slaps and then runs harder and thinks of nothing save for his steps, which he numbers and re-numbers each time he loses count, an annoying habit from his days in high school marching band that has suddenly become useful. *Fifty-seven, fifty-eight.* He is falling into a rhythm now, sweating profusely and not thinking, not thinking, really *not thinking.*

He catches the riverside trail at the carousel, closed up behind garage doors at this early hour, and runs east along the paved path toward the dog park, the university, and the mountains. He is not in good shape, but he has goals. One of these days he will reach the base of Mount Sentinel and run the switchbacks behind the university up to the M the way the football team does—but for now he will only jog to the Bark Park at Jacob's Island, catch his breath, and turn back. It's the goalsetting that makes the running possible.

The sun is surpassing the mountains, dazzling the river water as it plunges around the pylons of the Madison Street Bridge and the wide concrete footbridge suspended beneath it. A homeless man is sitting on a mat, reading a paperback. He's on his knees leaning forward like a Muslim at prayer. Beside him is a bicycle with a cardboard "For Sale" sign propped against it. The man does not look up as Dan passes and Dan does not look back.

A truck rumbles overhead like weather and the concrete of the footbridge undulates beneath him. Ahead of him, on one of the bridge pillars, a scrawl of graffiti says "Free from what?" and he doesn't recognize the woman in the tight shorts and sports bra until she says, "Hey Dan!"

He turns his head as she passes, says, "Hey," and nearly trips over his shoes. *Carolyn Lakes.* He's never seen her outside the high school before and isn't in fact entirely convinced he's seen her just now.

He quickens his pace, but it's no use—he is full of thoughts. He crosses the small bridge onto the grassy island that constitutes the dog park. He gasps for air. His shirt is soaked through. He looks, out of habit, across the river. On the far bank an apartment complex is going up. He wonders whether he actually saw her, Carolyn Lakes.

You are being stupid. You are a grown-ass man. You are married. It is inordinately stupid, this crush he's been harboring, the stirring he felt at hearing his name on her lips. A collie ambles past him to urinate in the brush.

He is running again and his mind is time, distance, pain, Carolyn. No, not Carolyn. He is thinking of nothing. He is running back the way he came, he is about to hit a stride, he can feel it, any second now, except he has come again to the footbridge and he stumbles wondering whether he will pass her once more. He wonders at the possibility of another hello, another glimpse, and now his eyes are searching for it, that hello, farther up the path and down each side street, glancing and glancing until Carolyn Lakes has become as God was to he and Sarah during those days of rhythmic happiness: everywhere at once and apt to appear at any moment.

Focus, you asshole. He skips an interval of walking and pushes harder to force silence on his mind, *time, distance, pain,* but his body, for the moment, has stopped registering pain. His thoughts have become muddled, his run has become muddled. He begins to feel omnipresently angry, angry in all directions, angry at the mountains. He hocks a gob of snot at the pavement and runs on past the shops and under the railroad tracks, a dizziness, an anger, but no pain, and now he is passing the garden and the cemetery and nearing the house—*not thinking, not thinking, twenty-two, twenty-three*—is turning into the neighborhood, is turning down the street, can see the house, is running as hard as his legs will allow, pushing until all he can feel is the pump of blood in his ears, a burning in his thighs—

***Listen, Dan, I was** a bastard. I'm saying that at the outset. I was a bastard and I don't blame her for how things shook out. We shouldn't've done it, but I had the money for the ring and we were moving in together anyway and the sex was good, and shit, what did we know? We were kids. We thought it made sense. So. It was good for a while, the novelty of it, you know all about that, the nudity and the decorating, but we didn't want to change. I shouldn't speak for her: I didn't want to change. That's what got us. We did our things. I drank too much, hell, we both drank too much, but it wasn't that, it was that she stopped wanting to ride on the motorcycle and I hate cats. I truly do. I hated every cloying name she had for those creatures and the house smelled like piss. But it wasn't the fighting that did us in—hell, every time we fought, we had sex, so the fighting was good actually. What got us was we quit fighting and became roommates.*

    —although, I'll tell you, if she were here on the line, she'd say it's cause I was a bastard. So there's two theories for you, and they both might be worth ponderin'. Call me back—I'm in town.

He comes gasping through the back door, all need and no feeling, thirsty for air and fumbling through the cupboard for a glass. He drinks a glass of water standing at the sink, then fills it again and sits down at the table to drink the second more slowly. When he finishes the glass he sets it in the sink. His cellphone begins to vibrate. It rattles against the countertop. A call from his brother. He ignores it.

He meets Sarah on the stairs on his way to the shower. She barely makes eye contact. In the kitchen the coffee pot is brimming and hot and calling out.

"Good morning."

"Good morning."

She kisses him, a peck, and slides past, is gone, no further contact between herself and his sweaty body. She does this every day and it baffles him, a cold clammy good morning and then a smudge of her chapstick like a variable he can't solve for.

He puzzles over it as he showers, the usual lines of speculation: she loves him or is still in the habit of loving him or the gesture is a remnant of who they used to be, a vestigial tail. He can hear his brother: "You've got to try a little tenderness. That's what she wants. I know that sounds like a shitty Michael Bublé song, but sometimes women need a little Bublé, you know?"

Oh shut up. Some mornings the kiss is enough. Today it has pissed him off.

Sarah is reading the comics in the newspaper but she does not look amused. In her green polo she looks like a younger version of herself: Sarah's First Job, After School Sarah, Sarah Earns A Little Spending Money—except her lips are too clenched, her brow too bent, for the illusion of youth to hold. It is beyond him why she's taken another semester off from teaching at the university (the teaching opportunity was the reason they'd moved back to Missoula) only to turn around and take a job pressing shirts at a dry cleaner's. He worries if she doesn't accept some courses for the fall the university will find another adjunct to fill their needs. In this hipster town every waitress is qualified to teach freshman comp.

"How's Ziggy?"

"Same old. The mouse is complaining that he doesn't keep enough cheese in the fridge. 'Not enough variety.'" She looks up at him through the steam of her coffee as he pours himself a bowl of Cap'n Crunch. Those blank brown eyes. "How was the run?"

"Uneventful. I made okay time. How did you sleep?"

"Fine," she says, lying also. He felt her jolt awake at—was it three? Maybe four. What does it matter. She looks down at her *Missoulian* and turns to the horoscopes. Dan returns to his cereal and swallows back an if-only.

When he stands to carry their empty cups and dishes to the sink he makes a decision. He jiggles the keys to the Subaru from his pants pocket and clunks them onto the table—a mistake, too aggressive, he sees her spine straighten. But he has already made up his mind. *Be chipper! Be cheerful!*

"I was thinking we should switch it up today," he says. "How about you drop me off at work this morning?"

"I'd rather not."

The response is immediate, no gap of consideration—it comes like a stab. She must see this on his face, because she adds, more gently, "Not with all the morning traffic. It will just be too much. This summer, when school lets out and things slow down. . . ."

Last time she'd said, no, not with all the ice on the roads, once it thaws, then we'll do it.

He picks up the keys. (*Be gentle.*) "Okay, well, are you ready to go?"

"I left my purse in the bedroom. I'll just be a minute."

He watches her jog up the stairs, her backside, and feels desire—or, if not desire, then the hollowed-out memory of it. Who the hell knows. As he heads for the garage he thinks again of Carolyn Lakes jogging by.

At school he is distracted all morning. He keeps skipping steps in his proofs and having to double back. Carson Hess nods off in the third row, the room is too warm, and in the middle of his uninspired mini-lecture on triangles he snaps at Mikaela Barbour, one of his best, most earnest students: "Something you'd like to share with the class?"

"I was only asking what page we're on."

He says, "One seventy-eight," and turns back to the chalkboard.

He was wrong, though, to single out Mikaela. He knows it and she more-than-knows-it. If teenagers known anything, they know when they've been wronged, and this includes even Mikaela Barbour who aspires to the Ivy Leagues out east. She sulks through the period, offering no answers to the questions she normally would have leapt at, and the other students stare on like livestock. She won't forgive him, but she'll forget over the weekend and return to her normal honor roll self come Monday. *Forget and forgive,* that's how it goes.

The bell rings and the students cast their assignments on his desk in a messy pile. He moves upstream through the students to nudge Carson awake. The boy starts and scurries off. Dan stoops to pick up a pencil. He begins straightening the desks.

"Hey."

He picks up a crumpled note, then turns to see Derek leaning in the doorway, tall and broad-shouldered, always at ease, the good-looking brother. He's charmed Nancy and Doris at the front desk again, and this time he isn't even wearing the visitor's badge. The lanyard is trailing out the back pocket of his jeans.

"How you doing? You get my message?"

"Haven't had a chance to listen to it yet."

Though he's barely a year older than Derek, Dan has always thought of him as his much younger brother. Never settled down, has never stuck with a job or a girl for more than a season. In the summers he'd always gone where the wildfires were, frontline work with the forest service in Colorado and California as well as Montana, and in the off-season he would waft through the bars in Missoula like a fat winter fly.

Occasionally he built furniture, had built Dan and Sarah's dining room table as a wedding present back before the really heavy drinking, which—at least according to what Dan keeps hearing from their mother—has finally subsided. Dan finds this hard to believe, but then he's always been quick to judge sweet innocent Derek. When he heard he'd wrecked the motorcycle Dan had assumed he'd been drinking. Not so. Derek had been heading *to* the bars, not from. A Range Rover pulled out in front of him and Derek slid into it going forty or fifty miles an hour. No metal frame, no seatbelt, no airbag, just a helmet—the crash should have killed him. He'd fractured half the bones in his body, including his skull, and was in a coma for a week. For six months he was laid up at St. Pat's. He'll walk with a limp for the rest of his life, but he has no memory of the accident and is due for a big settlement check and is jolly about the windfall. He likes to slap his leg and say, "I wrestled with the angels."

When it became clear that Derek was not going to die and would, in fact, recover almost completely, Dan struggled to sustain a feeling of sympathy—the fruits of a reckless life, he kept thinking—but Sarah had pushed him to have more compassion and he'd asked God to soften his heart.

Three months later, at the funeral luncheon for Sam, he watched Derek hobble over to Sarah on his crutches and whisper something in her ear that made her smile and cry all at once. In that moment Dan's lack of sympathy hardened into loathing. It was as if his brother, by living, had robbed him.

Derek takes an eraser from the chalk tray and begins wiping off the board. "I was over at the smokejumper base seeing if I could shake loose some teaching work. Those who can't do, right?" He gives his bum leg a pat. "I'm serious though, *teaching*. Gotta get out of Mom and Dad's house. I'm desperate."

"Any luck?"

"Hell no. They don't even have any openings. I knew it was a long shot."

"I'm sorry to hear that, but I've got another class coming in. You had to tell me this now?"

"Well you don't return my calls."

"I've been busy."

"Okay, but really, how have you been?"

"Busy."

Some months back Derek, cooped up and convalescing in his childhood bedroom, had decided to make Dan's marriage his new hobby. It started with phone calls and long voicemails, then quickly progressed to surprise classroom visits: "Hey, you gotta eat anyway, let's grab lunch."

Married at twenty-one and divorced at twenty-three, Derek was, by his own estimation, the wiser and more learned of the McDermott brothers, well versed in the ways of Failed Marriage and (doubly annoying) quite open about all his mistakes. What he's really doing (to Dan this seems obvious) is using Dan's troubles to make sense of his own wrecked life. A clear case of displacement or projection or whatever (Sarah would know the term).

"What I'd really like to do," says Derek, "is come and see Sarah some evening. I imagine she still must feel like a pile of shit."

Dan squares a desk in the back row. "She's getting along."

"Well I'd still like to see her."

"Send me a text message. We'll get something on the calendar."

"Tell her I want to come by and see how's she doing. I'm gonna bring a hot dish. A hot dish for a hot dish, you tell her I said that. It'll make her smile."

"Can we talk about this later? I'll call you."

Derek smiles. "Yeah, you'll call me."

Students are beginning to trickle into the classroom. Derek puts the eraser on the chalk tray and eases into the hall. Ainsley Breckenridge eyes him as he goes, then nudges Kelly Bruce, and they giggle. Dan leafs backward through his teaching notes. The bell rings and the students settle into the desks. A fat fly makes a long, slow lap around the ceiling.

Carolyn Lakes sits on the far side of the teachers' lounge with an old copy of *The New Yorker* in her lap. One hand rests on the page, the other makes gestures in the air as she speaks with the art teacher. Her nails are painted pink.

Dan sits down at the table across the room with a carton of strawberry milk, a microwaved cup of noodles, and a stack of ungraded quizzes. He takes the first quiz and begins making Xs with a red pen, and he thinks, how strange, the musicality of her voice, the jolt he would feel if she were to suddenly ask him what he thought. They were talking about a home design show.

The art teacher gets up and says goodbye, and now the room is silent except for the rustle of Dan's papers, the slurp of a noodle. When Carolyn looks up from her magazine and says hello, Dan's reaction is delayed—he almost looks over his shoulder to see who she's talking to, but no, she is talking to *him*. She has the carriage of a former college athlete and the confidence that comes with it: square shoulders, toned limbs, perfect posture, direct and sustained eye contact, levelled suddenly at Dan. He nearly knocks over his milk carton.

"I didn't know you ran."

"Oh I don't. Much. I'm just getting into it."

"Well, it's never too late to start." She leans forward. "I'm signed up for a marathon in September. I've done two halves before, but never a full one. I'm a little nervous."

"I'm sure you'll do fine."

"We'll see. The first half-marathon I did, I puked my guts out at the end."

He laughs—inconceivable, Carolyn Lakes, throwing up.

She smiles. "You think that's funny?"

"Oh, no, no, I'd be in worse shape than that. I get winded just going from the footbridge to the dog park."

"Well you should keep at it. You'd be surprised what a body can endure." She pauses, leans back, and glances down at her magazine. He assumes the conversation is over, but then she continues, "I was just reading this article about a guy who got struck by lightning and died. He was dead for like, three minutes, and he had this out-of-body experience where he watched a woman resuscitate him—which, you know, take it or leave it, but the interesting thing is that after, when he went back to living his life, he started hearing all this beautiful music in his head. Everywhere he went. It was so beautiful he bought a piano and taught himself to play—he'd never studied music in his life—just so he could get that music out of his head."

Dan does not know what to say to this. He says, "That's pretty crazy."

"Apparently, according to the author, it's called 'sudden musicophilia,' which is a cool word, right? *Musicophilia*. The guy says he thinks his life was spared because of the music, like it had been inside him all along and was supposed to come out and that's why he didn't stay dead."

"Are his songs any good?"

She frowns. "I don't know. The article didn't say." She takes a sip of her green smoothie and thinks for a moment. "I guess I assumed the music must be pretty decent. I mean, otherwise, why write the article?"

"That's a good point. You're probably right."

She stands and she nods. The matter has been settled. "All right, I'm off to run some copies. Have a good one, Dan."

"You too."

As he gathers up the refuse of his lunch, it hits him: he's happy. He heads into the hallway and the fluorescent light on the linoleum feels a little less garish. The bell rings, and as the students flood the hall like ants he knows he will be kind to his afternoon classes, kind to Mikaela Barbour on Monday, kind to Sarah tonight and all weekend.

That was all he needed, just to be talked to. To be noticed. Carolyn has talked to him. Carolyn has noticed him. Perhaps now he can be at peace while he waits for the old Sarah to return. Now that Carolyn has noticed him perhaps he can stop thinking about Carolyn.

Perhaps, he thinks, and he thinks of her throughout the afternoon.

On his way from the driveway to the door, Dan makes up his mind to sweep Sarah into a bear hug. He moves through the living room to the kitchen, through the smell of stuffed peppers, and feels the energy building within him. He turns the corner and hugs her from behind. He lifts her up off the ground and kisses her on the neck—*the old days!*—but her body goes stiff, hard to hold. He puts her back down.

She says, "You almost made me spill the lettuce."

He turns away. He is feeling good for once and he never gets to feel good anymore. He notices, as if for the first time, the white walls of the house, the little nail holes where the photos once hung. After the funeral she'd said, "I just can't," and at the time that had sounded like a good argument—he'd helped her box them all up. Now he's not sure. Without the pictures the house feels off. It's as if they've just moved in.

"You know what," he says, still trying, "we should paint one of these walls. Like blue or turquoise. Something bright. An accent wall."

"Yeah," she says as she begins chopping carrots for the salad. The blade thwacks against the cutting board.

If they paint that may give him a chance to ask about putting some pictures back up. Not all of them, of course, but a few, a little of that old happiness, pale and watered down, sure, but something.

"What about light orange? Or peach? Or peach with green stripes like those boxers I have? We're not renting, we could do anything."

"It would be so much work, Dan. Think how much furniture we'd have to move."

"No, it'd be the work of a weekend. It'd be fun. What can I be doing to help with dinner?"

"You can go and sit down. It'll be ready in a minute."

He walks into the dining room but does not sit down. He looks from wall to wall imagining the room with the trim around the windows a misty shade of blue. Sarah sets the peppers and the salad on the table by the water pitcher. "Can we eat?"

"Let's eat."

She sits. She bows her head. When she lifts her eyes to the serving dish, Dan says, "I think blue would be good."

"Stop it. I said I don't want to." She glops a stuffed pepper onto his plate. A wave of spice hits his eyes.

"Listen, I'm sorry I came up behind you like that. I shouldn't have done it. I was just looking forward to seeing you is all. Can we start over?"

She looks at him and, through what seems to be an act of sheer will, untenses the muscles in her neck. "I had a bad day. It's not your fault. I shouldn't have snapped at you like that. You're right, we got off on the wrong foot."

"What happened to make your day bad?"

She thinks for a moment. "A couple customers gave me a hard time. I don't want to re-live it." *Every day is bad.* "How was your day?"

"It was all right."

"Just all right? You were ebullient a minute ago."

"Yeah, well, you know how excited I get when I get to tell teenagers about triangles."

"Yeah," she says, but doesn't tease or roll her eyes.

"At lunch today I heard about this man who got struck by lightning. Apparently after they resuscitated him he had to buy a piano and learn to play because he was full of music."

"Sounds like bullshit." She looks down at her plate. He quells something that has risen inside of him. She looks up. "I'm sorry, Dan. God, it's like I don't know how to be a person anymore."

"It's all right. The peppers are good."

"They're not, but it's nice of you to say so."

After dinner Dan rises, sniffling from the peppers, and he begins to collect the dishes. So much silence—it is a relief to be standing. Before the accident there'd been so much to talk about: Sam, of course, but also books and shows, the people that they knew, local politics, sermons, gossip, funny stories, the things they would do the next weekend. They used to be people who made plans and marked calendars.

As he stacks the plates, Sarah takes a thin book of poems from a shelf and retreats to her wingback chair. After a minute she closes the book and puts Netflix on the TV. She scrolls through the options and scrolls for a long time. She turns off the TV. "I'm heading to bed."

This early? "Okay. I'll be up." As he places the dishes in the machine his phone twitches in his pocket, a text message from Derek: "Sry for comin at a bad time 2day. Lemme kno about visiting. any excuse to get out of the house = good."

When he goes up to the bedroom he knows he'll find Sarah asleep already, or pretending to be. He'll kiss her on the cheek, switch off the lamp, and start counting while the train cars rumble, another step in a journey toward a horizon they'll never reach.

As he scrubs the cheese from the big casserole dish he thinks again of Carolyn Lakes and the man who was struck by lightning. He replays their conversation in his mind, and now he is thinking about talking with her again in the teachers' lounge on Monday, about greeting her as they pass on the bridge, river below, cars above, just talking. Just talking, and she will be smiling. It doesn't even seem like a stretch.

iii. silences

There are moments when the sobs come heaving up unexpected (this is desirable), but more and more she has to seek them out. Sitting on the little bed is still a reliable method, but standing in the doorway has ceased to be effective. Too often now she turns the knob intending to grieve and finds she can only stand in the room and pretend to cry. *What's wrong with you? Don't you care?*

What she likes about the laundromat is the sound of the machines, the soft godless tumble of shirts and socks, the warm humming mixed with the mingled smells of soap and lint, how the sun through the plate glass cooks it all into one thing, one texture, a sound that fills and empties her, lulling like waves rinsing the shore. It blots her out. In her dreams she sees the washer drums turning, the clothes gasping up from the suds and plunging again, and sometimes she believes she is awake.

She stirs. The scrape of stubble on her cheek, a light touch from his chapped lips. She lies still. He hums, is humming, a little jingle from a radio commercial. She has told him a thousand times she hates it when he hums, but he never realizes that he's doing it. He hums as he changes into gym shorts and jaunts down the stairs. When the back door thumps shut she rolls over. She takes the prayer book from the night stand and gets down on her knees: God has gone up with a shout, the Lord with the sound of the ram's horn. Sing praises to God, sing praises. Sing praises to our King, etc.

She rises to get dressed, black slacks, green polo, and as she surveys the shoes piled in her closet she thinks, *You could live without them.* Same for the dresses, *You don't need them.* More and more she is asking *how much?* and *how many?* When she hears Dan on the stairs she shuts the closet and heads down to meet him, a Judas kiss, and she keeps going. She used to love the front window, the way it lets light pool in the living room, good for the plants though it's faded the quilt. Now the sun through the window fills the house with a watery light that makes all her things look cheap, the wine crates along the walls that are shelves for her books, the frayed upholstery on her wingback chair, the decorative birdcage slotted with mail, mostly junk. Only the hardiest of the plants have survived the winter, the succulents which need no care and the peace lily that collapses in a sulk when it goes too long without water. The orchids and herbs on the TV stand have all withered. Someone ought to pull up the stalks and stuff them in the garbage.

In the kitchen, as she spreads open the paper, she recalls the last conversation she had with her friend Bethany: "You can't just sit—you have to keep moving. Work in the garden if you feel like you can't write. You need to stay active." It will be a good line to throw in Bethany's face when Sarah shows up on her doorstep, duffle in hand: "I can't just sit. I have to keep moving. You said."

Bethany checks in with her every week with a phone call. She has a six-year-old girl and a four-year-old boy and she knows nothing about loss.

Dan bops down the stairs. "How's Ziggy?"

Fuck Ziggy. "He's getting by."

"Glad to hear it."

He empties the last drizzle of milk onto his cereal. He sits down at the table, then stands again because he forgot a spoon. He does not interrupt as she reads the morning's Dear Abby ("Racy Facebook Profile Makes Grandma Look Askance"), but the whole time she can feel his eyes on her face like a gnat. Is he humming again? She thought he was, but now she hears nothing. Op-ed pull quote of the day: "Only Israel can break the cycle—you can't expect terrorists to start holding bake sales and building new roads."

His spoon scrapes the bottom of the bowl and he jingles the keys from his pocket. To the garage, to the car. She stares out the window at the houses ticking by.

In this vehicle (the one not destroyed) parenthood still clings to them like an odor. Dan removed the car seat and stowed it in the basement, but the smell of animal crackers is ground deep into the seat cushions. That juice stain in the back? Permanent. Five years ago it wasn't a thing she'd thought she'd wanted, a slobbery creature tugging her sleeve crying "Mommy!" She'd seen too many men dump the kids with the wife at church picnics and MFA cookouts, had watched gifted friends like Bethany forfeit careers that were only just beginning.

She herself was midway through her master's thesis when pregnancy came looming like the snuffer at the end of an acolyte's crook—six days and still no period. Was it the stress? Her advisor, a dour poet laureate visiting from New England, had axed seven poems with her defense just four weeks off and she was drowning in comp papers. An anovulatory cycle wasn't out of the question, but with her luck and God's wry sense of timing she wasn't going to be surprised if she woke up in the morning with the urge to vomit.

She was especially irritated with Dan because she was the one who'd miscalculated. He'd offered to run out for more condoms, but no, she'd said no, I checked the calendar, we're fine. They were in the moment and this was much needed thesis sex. It wasn't until the next morning she realized she'd stopped updating that calendar. Natural family planning, she'd had herself convinced she was on the cutting edge of feminism, rejecting birth control chemicals to embrace and understand the natural rhythms of her own body. How could she have been such a granola?

Dan sympathized, he really did, but he was insufferable, he couldn't hide it, his chest was puffed out. Every cup of tea he brought her as she graded came with a stupid grin.

"You know what would make you feel better?"

"Don't say it."

She waited for a sure sign of what the future held, but none came. No morning sickness, no menstruation. She defended her thesis, tolerated her parents at the post-graduation cook out, and . . . nothing. It wasn't until a week later, as she and Dan were settling into the summer, packing boxes for their move up to Kalispell (Dan had been hired full-time at a middle school) that her period returned.

That was that, a weight lifted, normalcy returned—except now she felt annoyed. It happened as if overnight: Missoula became a town pimpled with babies, regal babies in bicycle-drawn chariots, wobbling toddlers with their fists in their mouths, red infants mewing at church in those cute little hats. It was disgusting—she wanted one. In her notebook she wrote, *Glory be to God for diapered things, spattered 'cross the city like rose-moles in all stipple upon trout that spawn.*

She said to Dan, "I changed my mind."

"Really?"

"Yes."

They chose a room in the new house and christened it the nursery because they assumed it would take only one or two tries. If they'd learned anything in public school, it was that every romantic encounter is fraught with the potential for pregnancy—but for her and Dan this was not so.

"We could get a dog," Dan suggested, five months in.

"We are not settling for a *dog*."

She poured over her granola books on fertility, bought new ones, made adjustments, petitioned God daily. Eight months more and she got the Lord to capitulate. They conceived. The whole thing was a story they'd tell when they got old and wise, but in the moment it was strange, she was growing a person. She'd always known, in the abstract, it was possible, but now—! Their love had become a person, a small human was inside her, no bigger than a goldfish, but the doctor was quite confident it was a person. "There's a leg," she said, tapping a grey blob on the ultrasound screen. "Do you see it?"

"Oh yeah," said Dan, and Sarah said, "Yeah, me too," though she wasn't quite sure. The gel was cold on her stomach, and she strained her neck to look closer.

In the weeks before the accident she'd been hoping he'd bring it up, another baby. Conceiving had been hard, she didn't want to try again—but part of her, a growing part, had wanted him to talk her into it.

"Today's your long day, right?" It might be the first thing he's said to her all morning. She can't remember.

"Yeah."

"I was thinking I'd make minestrone for dinner. Would that be all right?"

"Yeah."

"That and some garlic bread. You can't go wrong with garlic bread."

"Garlic bread solves everything."

The shops and restaurants stream by. Another minute and they'll be there.

"Is there anything else I could do?"

"I think with the bread the soup will be plenty."

"That's not— Minestrone it is."

He pulls into the handicap spot, then reaches over the armrest for his awkward hug. "I love you," he says, and she speaks the response.

Through the plate glass of the laundromat she can see Mandy Merritt at the register, the top of her head as she fills the cash drawer: a white line of scalp through that black-purple hair. She's dashing a roll of pennies against the counter like a stubborn egg. *How many times have I told her what a pain it is to re-roll those pennies? We never use them.* Sarah pushes through the door, and Mandy looks up.

"Hey there, Mrs. McD!"

"Good morning."

Mandy's eye contact lingers too long, too hopeful. A fleck of blue-grey lint stands out against the dye-job like dandruff, and Sarah suppresses a mother's urge to pluck it as she slips past the counter to head for the presses.

This much in Mandy's favor: she started the machines when she came in so there's already a load waiting to be pressed. The best part of the job, in Sarah's opinion, is removing the clothes from the big pistachio-colored machines and pressing them on their designated presses. There is a press specifically designed to smooth out cuffs and collars, a gentler one for blouses, this one just for slacks. A puff of steam as she brings down the lid and there it is—a perfect crease down the leg. It's soothing. She does not want to stare at a sea of faces and teach them rhetoric. Her students and colleagues had all been so contemptibly sympathetic, kind e-mails, soft faces. Flowers. But she couldn't bear to be alone in the house all day either. This was a good compromise. From the presses in the back Sarah can look out at the shabby sunlit houses across the street and watch the people come and go unaware of her existence—the mailman in blue shorts, the Mormons in their impossibly white shirts, the old woman with the terrier stooping now to bag the dog's poop.

Two or three of the college-aged girls working at the laundromat have recognized Sarah from the university, one even asked where to go for a drop/add slip, but mostly they take the hint and let her be—all of them except Mandy, Mandy with the eggplant hair.

The girl is a great misreader of social cues, always chatting up customers who would rather be watching the muted talk show on the television in the corner or reading from the book they have open in their laps. She is quick to listen to anything that seems like advice and is always petitioning Sarah for female mentorship, inserting her ex-boyfriend and class schedule ungracefully into their small exchanges: "What's the difference between psychology and sociology?" "Corey has a new girlfriend," "Are night classes hard?" Every interaction with her feels sticky. Beneath her *Hey there's* and *How are ya's* Sarah can sense a yawning insecurity, a thirst for encouragement. (If she asked outright, "Will you read them?" Sarah would said no and that would be the end of it. Saying no to Mandy would be easy, people can't be healed by other people, not really, and maybe deep down Mandy knows that. Maybe that's why she won't ask outright for what she wants).

For a while there was a man who came in every Friday. He would come in in the mid-morning with a small stack of pants and shirts to be washed and pressed and just barely enough socks and undershirts to fill a top loader. He was inept but kind, handsomely grey about the temples, and fit, perhaps in his mid-forties, perhaps older. She suspected he was recently divorced. He could never seem to get the dryers to read the magnetic strip on his swipe card.

One day, while she was helping him with his card, he asked for her number—"in case, you know, I ever get a dryer of my own one day, ha ha"—and she told him she was married. The man blushed and apologized. She told him she needed to go press some pants.

The man did not return, not even to pick up his dry cleaning. He vanished from the world, but the idea of him lingered. Not the idea of an affair, but the idea of giving up and starting over. As soon as she thought of it, it felt right, the best thing for her and Dan both, fresh starts at the lives they have left. They're not so old. And sure, she knows Jesus spoke against divorce in the New Testament, but that had been in a culture where a woman without a husband had no way of supporting herself, and what's more, her own parents seemed happier for their divorce (though she'd always resented them that happiness).

No, it will hurt him at first, but in the long run he will be happier. She is going to leave him *because* she loves him, because he will never leave her, the stupid grieving mother who— How could he? He is a good man. He has no options. She will set him free—that's how she presents the plan to God in her prayers, though it seems impossible for her to know for sure what her own true motives are. Perhaps she is only being selfish. That's the answer she often thinks she hears in God's silence.

She drapes a pair of slacks on a hanger and reaches into the machine for another. If she's being honest, the reason she'd shown that initial kindness to the divorced man was that he'd reminded her a little of an older, more stately version of Dan. Dan had always had an endearing clumsiness about him. An orderly thinker in a chaotic world, when he knocks over a water glass in a restaurant (not uncommon) he is always delayed by a moment of disbelief before he starts mopping up the spill. It is as if he can't fathom how such a thing could happen. He's always been bumbling but bumbling in a way that underscores his gentleness. Truth be told, his ham-fisted attempts to cheer her up—the loud talking, the ill-timed mas-sages, the urgings to get back behind the wheel—these were really just distortions of a thing she used to find attractive.

But this is not a helpful thought. She smothers it as it rises with a deep breath of fabric-softened air as Mandy flips the CLOSED sign to OPEN. A gust of wind might strand that girl in a tree. She's bird-like petite with a round face, and the angle of her wide drawn-on eyebrows doesn't help. She wears too much makeup, thick purple mascara, is only just learning how to use it or is compensating for the loss of the love of Corey. Maybe both. She bobs through the rows of washers, opening each porthole door just an inch to make the machines (her words) "more inviting."

Sarah looks out the window at the sparrows on the powerline, and Mandy appears at her side.

"I think I might be gluten intolerant." She blurts this out, nervous-like, as she pulls a blouse from the machine.

"Mmm."

The front bell rings—startles Mandy—and a frazzled looking woman appears at the counter with garment bags stacked high in her arms. Before Sarah can even suggest it, Mandy is turning. "Hey! How can I help you?"

Was it only yesterday that she found Mandy's poems in her purse? It was, only yesterday. The sun was slick across the shop windows when she pushed out the door for lunch, and she had to stop for a moment to let her eyes adjust to the light.

The mountains were dire drought yellow, or would have been if the grass here wasn't always dire drought yellow regardless of rainfall, and she was reminded again that, though she's lived in Montana ten years, she will always be an easterner at heart. She still catches herself longing for the mountains to turn Appalachian green in the springtime, is still surprised when she steps outside into a town that smells like campfire smoke. Could she smell it now? She thought she could. She knew, from *The Missoulian*, that the first wildfire of the season was growing, not shrinking, out in Idaho. She thought maybe the city had already begun to take on its perpetual summer haze. She couldn't prove it, but she could feel it. It was May. The days were coming when the dog walkers of Missoula would be shrouded in milky sunlight, and still they will walk their dogs. Dan, who grew up in Montana, never seems to notice the smoke until little flakes of ash start landing on cars.

Across the street the kids at Hellgate High were also slipping out for lunch, moving in packs toward the restaurants up the block. The school is a red-brick tower, something like a cross between a castle and a pizza oven and nothing like Sentinel High, just a mile south, with its sprawling lawns and broad flat windows where Dan was probably right now dabbing mayonnaise from his beard, his brow furrowed as he corrected a stack of quizzes.

As she waited for the traffic light to change she watched a cocky-looking boy puff on a cigarette as he talked down to a mousy-looking girl. She imagined herself asking the boy for a smoke to shut him up. She imagined taking a deep drag, eyes closed, and then spooling a long stream into the air—she'd done it before, cigars at poker nights, pilfered cigarettes in high school with her boyfriend behind the band shell at the park, that deep satisfaction of doing something defiant and self-destructive.

At the bistro she ordered a salad, then filled a mason jar with lemon water and sat down by the window. As she slipped her wallet into her purse her hand brushed a wad of papers not hers. What was it? She took it out and laid it on the table, a wedge of printer paper folded into quarters, too thick to lie flat at the crease. It gaped at her like a sock puppet.

The sun shone through a corner of the top sheet, and she could see text centered on the page, a curlicue font, and she knew without looking any further that these were Mandy's poems—because of course they were Mandy's poems, of course Mandy is a bashful closeted poet imposing herself, seeking affirmation. Of course. "You're a writing teacher and I like writing," she'd said during their first shared shift. "We must have a lot in common." A poet. Sarah had known it all along without knowing it, and now, waiting for her Caesar salad, she felt a tug at the hem of her teacher's soul. *Take a look.*

The poems would be bad but not *entirely* bad, and that's what made them dangerous. Somewhere in that tangle of sentimentality and cliché, hidden like a sliver of glass in shag carpet, would be a fragment of youthful promise: a compelling image, a startling juxtaposition—a teachable moment. If the girl cared enough to reverse pickpocket her work into Sarah's handbag, odds were she wasn't completely devoid of potential. In writing quite a lot could be accomplished simply by giving a damn.

So she knew what would happen if she looked. She'd experienced it a dozen times in grad school, camped out at Liquid Planet or the Break Café with a stack of student essays on her left and a half-eaten bear claw on her right, three cups of coffee chewing on her stomach. She'd be ready to call it quits and go home, the lines blurring together on the page—and then she'd find one, a One True Sentence, and she'd pick up her pen, lean forward, and cut through the sloppy freshman syntax out to that glimmer in the weeds.

She was, or had been, one of those foolish teachers cursed with the belief that good writing could be taught if someone was willing to point the student in the right direction, and now she could hear Bethany in her head, interpreting her experience: This is a prompting from the Spirit, a call to respond, an invitation to have compassion on this kid who (be honest) you a little bit hate. *Good writing can be taught if there's someone willing to point the way.*

She was not willing. She greeted the waiter as he set the salad on the table, and with the back of her hand she batted the pages to the floor. *Not today,* she told God, and then she bowed her head to thank Him for her food.

When she finished the salad she did not stoop to the floor, she did not pick up the poems, and she did not return the poems to her purse—but after lunch when she hung her bag on the hook in the break room she found that the wad of poetry was still there in the guts of her bag. It sat there slightly open, like a child with its arms stretched out, waiting to be picked up.

There were natural explanations. She might've knocked the poems off the table and back into her bag. Or this was a second wad that she'd missed the first time. *This doesn't have to be significant.*

God, as usual, said nothing, though she thought she felt him watching. The front bell rang, a customer at the counter. She stuffed the poems back into her purse, down between her sunglasses and her tampons. *So be it, but not today.*

The sky is bruise-purple when Sarah starts home. The bistro up the street is empty, the high school looks now like a prison. The sun is spilling orange on the river.

On the far side of the Higgins Street Bridge the marquee above the Wilma boasts a band she's never heard of. A long line of people are waiting to get in, ripped denim, black tee shirts, the smell of pot. Mostly men in their thirties. "Hey baby," says one, and his friends laugh. *Fuck you.* She ignores them as she walks by.

The bars are filling with dinner crowds and the coffee shops are emptying out. A grad student with disheveled hair emerges from a café clutching a satchel and squinting like a mole as he shuffles into the twilight. In an alcove up the street a one-armed man is playing a guitar. His dirty fingers hammer hard against the frets, a flamenco-sounding tune.

She makes her way northwest through the town to the tunnel beneath the railroad tracks. Things are quieter on the other side. There's the community garden and houses with front lawns, a steady rumble from the highway, but not so many people, a few on their porches, some kids in a yard.

Sarah walks up the porch, braces herself, then steps through the front door.

"There you are!" Dan calls from the kitchen. He's at the stove stirring the soup. His eyes are wild with restraint—she's worried him. "I thought I was gonna have to send out a search party!"

He turns for a hug, but she slips past him. She says, "The girl to replace me was an hour late, so I had to stay on. Something about she couldn't get her cousin's dog to take his Prozac. I didn't ask but she told me anyway. These girls are always coming in late."

He slides a pan of garlic bread into the oven. "You should've called."

"I did."

He frowns.

"Okay, yeah, I should've called. I didn't think I'd be that late. Do you need help?"

"It's all pretty much finished."

Good. "All right." She moves into the living room. She tosses her purse on the couch, then tips into her wingback chair and dangles her feet over the armrest. The table has been set. The soup spoons rest on paper napkins folded into triangles. The doorbell rings. "I'll get it," she says, standing up.

She opens the door, and the goateed pastor from the coffee shop church blinks at her. His name is Trent or Trevor or Chad. He is one of several associate pastors. He blinks again, then smiles with many teeth.

"Sarah! It's been a while since we've seen you at Peak Church. I thought I'd see how you two are doing. I brought a care package." He holds out a wicker basket full of bagels and coffee beans and a staple-bound book with a picture of the seashore on the cover, *Even There You Are With Me: Meeting God in the Midst of Grief.* Two carabiners dangle from the rim of the basket, each one printed with the church's mountain peak logo.

A second slowly passes. She says, "Well, come in."

The pastor steps into the living room and studies the Maryland state flag coasters on the end tables as Sarah shuts the door. When he sees that she has remained standing, he sets the basket on the couch and slides his hands into the pockets of his jeans. "It's been a while," he says again. "How are you two holding up?"

Dan appears in the doorway to the kitchen. "We've been attending St. Mark's Lutheran. It seems right for us. It's quieter, right for this season."

This season. She almost smiles. How many times has Dan listened to her rail against that Christian cliché? Here he is, deploying the phrase like a tank.

The pastor nods with deep sympathy. "I'm glad to hear you two are engaged in Christian community. It's so important to be connected with the Body when, well, you know, during times of trial." He nods at the basket. "Those bagels are from the local place. Should be fresh."

The timer on the oven begins to beep.

"Sounds like dinner's ready," Dan says, more to Sarah than to the pastor.

Sarah says, "It was nice of you to stop by."

"Could you use prayer? Are there specific ways Peak Church can be praying for you?"

The oven continues to beep.

"Honestly," says Dan, "we've got more prayer than we know what to do with, but we appreciate the offer. It was good of you to stop by." He slips back into the kitchen.

"Well, yes, and it's good to see you both doing well." He nods as he heads to the door. "Enjoy those bagels."

"We will," says Sarah. As she draws the deadbolt she looks back at Dan. He shrugs as he sets the garlic bread on the table, but it's a Han Solo shrug. He is pleased that he's pleased her.

"You sit down, I'll bring in the soup," she says.

"Just hurry back."

She shudders—he's going to make a pass at her. He's chased off the meddling pastor, now he's expecting a reward. She ladles the soup and clunks the bowls on the table. Before he can speak, she plops into her chair. "Today was a bad day."

"Yeah?" His eyes flash, and she sees he is holding back a sort of hunger.

"There's this one girl who never stops talking. A three-hour shift and she talked non-stop."

"That sucks."

"It does." She knows what he's doing, but also she finds that she wants to say more. She says, "All I want is to press clothes and put things on hangers. I don't want to *talk* about the clothes, and I don't want to *talk* about boys, and I certainly don't want to talk about her budding gluten allergy."

"It's worse than I thought."

He can never be kind without also being patronizing. She wants to say something wounding, but checks the urge. She says, "What about you? Was your day awful?"

"I've had better. I got it in my head today, though, that maybe I should sign up for a 5k. If you're not moving forward, you're falling behind, you know?"

What a vapid thing to say. She says nothing, and for a while they eat in silence. When he dips the last of his bread into the last of his soup the broth dribbles down his beard and she can't help herself. She reaches across the table with a napkin to wipe it from his chin. He laughs. "Listen, I'll do the rest of the cleanup—you go upstairs, take a bath or something. Enjoy some quiet."

"Maybe I will."

Enjoy some quiet. She feels the urge to do something destructive, and when she reaches the top of the stairs she stops at the door to Sam's bedroom. She considers going in but does not. Tonight she is too angry to feel sad—it would be a waste, more skin on the callous. So she continues up the hall to the bathroom. If she hurries she can be asleep (or faking it) before Dan finishes scrubbing the pot.

Tonight she's not quick enough—she is rubbing lotion on her elbows when he enters the room. He smiles at her and nods and makes a big show of saying nothing as he changes out of his clothes. He kisses her good night, turns off the lamp, and settles in on his side. He thinks he's found a winning strategy.

The next morning: a scratchy kiss, the shush of his drawers. As he dresses he bumps the blinds, setting them askew, and a bar of sun falls on her face. A warmth on her cheek, light shines through her eyelids, an orange-red glow.

She reaches for the prayer book: Come and listen, all you who fear God, and I will tell you what he has done for me.

She rises feeling restless, straightens the blinds and looks down at the yard, at the sunken rectangle that must once-upon-a-time have been a garden. It's Wednesday, her odd day off in the middle of the week, a desert of a day. Bethany's words: *keep moving.*

She used to spend hours in the garden at the old house in Kalispell. She'd slip the baby monitor into the pocket of her overalls and run her hands through the dirt while Sam napped and Dan taught, and lines from poems she'd read in the morning (she always tried to read one or two before Sam woke up) would come back to her as she worked, planting, weeding, pruning, picking.

She would turn those lines over like a smooth stone in her pocket as she examined the tomatoes and the zucchinis, and she would cobble together poems of her own, a line or two at a time. She would scratch them down quickly in a soil-smudged notebook, never knowing when Sam's cries might call her back to the house.

When she wrote something that particularly pleased her, she would tape a handwritten draft to the sliding glass door for Dan to see when he came home.

She hears Dan thump through the back door. He's lumbering around the kitchen. She digs to the bottom of her drawer for an old pair of jeans, then meets him on the stairs, kisses him, and continues down. It's bagels for breakfast. When he leaves she lingers over her coffee and takes a tentative stab at the crossword puzzle in the paper. Then, when the midmorning silence in the house is almost too much, she dumps the coffee in the sink and sets out.

Normally on Wednesdays she walks to the Safeway to buy groceries. Wandering through the products is a good way to kill time, but today she walks through the tunnel under the railroad tracks and up the street to a small garden shop where she buys what she can carry: some seed packets, a new hoe, and a cylindrical trellis for tomatoes.

Returning she finds a package on the porch. Bethany had said she was sending a book, "a book of poems! Can you believe it? I actually found some I *like*. I mean besides yours."

Hands full, Sarah flips the package across the threshold with her foot, then heads out back to the grassed-over scab that once was a garden. She drops the seeds and the trellis by the tree, then raises the hoe. Roots pop as she peels back the grass, and she works all morning at carving up the ground. She breaks briefly for lunch (a few carrots, some string cheese for protein), then goes back to it, bit by bit reclaiming the garden from the earth. She sweats and can feel for the first time in a long time the muscles in her arms. The chunks of sod begin to stack up.

When Dan finds her out back he says nothing. He ducks into the house and emerges in torn jeans and an old Blues Traveler t-shirt. He retrieves the old hoe from the garage, the one splinted together with duct tape and a garden stake, and without a word he joins her in the garden. He hacks and tugs at the ground, and though she tries not to be, she is aware of his love.

When the sun begins to smudge into the horizon they step back and look at what they've done: a crust of lawn piled up by the tree, dark folds of soil exposed. He suggests she shower first, and while she does he drives off to pick up a pizza from their old favorite place.

After he showers they put the pizza box on the coffee table and cycle through Netflix until they settle on an *X-Files* episode, one of the sillier ones, and for once, as the theme song plays, the silence between them feels easy. She rests her head on his shoulder and allows him to run his fingers through her hair. She tries not to think about what she is doing.

The next morning, when she wakes to the sound of her husband waking, she prays, "Lord, you have brought me in safety to this new day. Preserve me with your mighty power that I may not fall into sin nor be overcome by adversity, and in all I do direct me to the fulfilling of your purpose, through Jesus Christ my Lord, amen."

She meets Dan on the stairs, kisses him, then looks out at the garden and thinks of peppers, green and bell and habanero. When Dan comes down the stairs humming, she chides herself: It's foolish to think in future tense.

He drives her to work. They don't talk, and though it still feels all right, she senses the silence beginning to stale. Sooner or later someone (Dan) will break open the quiet.

But she sheds these concerns as she steps into the hum of the laundromat. This morning she is on a rare solo shift, just her and the machines. There is a woman in the corner watching a debate on *The View* ("Is Age-Shaming the New Fat-Shaming?"), and a younger woman is folding sweaters and skirts. To them Sarah is all but invisible. She presses the shirts, replenishes the bucket of free detergent, observes the Mormons on the sidewalk as they oil the chains on their bikes. There is an odd lightness in her body, as if she is expecting something good.

Her shift ends at two, and on her walk home she pauses halfway across the Higgins Street Bridge to look down at the water. There are kayakers in the river below taking turns in the little rapids, paddling and paddling but going nowhere, a liquid treadmill, "Brennan's Wave" is what they call it, after a person who died. People with children watch from park benches on the bank. Beyond them the carousel is turning, but she's too far off to hear the music.

In the backyard as she sprinkles seeds into the rows she feels something opening inside her, a desirous sort of emptiness: the desire to be writing.

She's scratched things down here and there, moody fragments, but nothing substantial, not in a long time. When she finishes with the seeds she goes upstairs, changes clothes, and sits down at her desk for the first time in months. She opens her notebook to a clean set of pages, holds her pen in her hand, takes a breath. Nothing comes. No words. She's untroubled. She has experienced this before, many times, the restless desire to be writing coupled with the absence of words. Reading often helps to break loose the language inside her.

She opens yesterday's package: *Sprigs of Sun* by Paulette Kinchla, disappointing but not surprising from Bethany, who's never had any ear for literature. Back in grad school, when Sarah was heavy into language poetry, she'd decided without reading any of her work that Kinchla was too popular to be good. But if she can subject herself to the horoscopes and the Dear Abbys every morning, she can give Paulette one try. She opens to the middle, reads aloud: "A lazy day, I make no apology. Let the leaves sweep the porch, let the poems roam the hillside. I didn't make this day. Neither did you." Not awful. She turns the page. The speaker walks on a stony beach. The smell of salt spray is evoked, and then, as if the sunshine has a hinge

> *Brady comes back, like a dove from a scarf,*
> *or a quarter from an ear, nothing like a memory:*
> *rays are catching in his curls, he is pleased with himself,*
> *it was all just a joke, "How clever am I?"*
> *and I only want to touch him and he only wants to run,*
> *and I know I will never, never ever catch up.*

Sarah closes the book. For a moment she listens. The silence, it feels okay. *It does.* She wills it to be so. She allows herself, guardedly, to remember the little ways that Sam filled the house—the smudges on the walls, the Legos in the dustpan, the roars and explosions his dinosaurs made as they fought, in retrospect a sort-of song and now she is even hoping for some small noise elsewhere in the house so that Sam might be given briefly back.

She often wakes in the night to the sound of the house settling and thinks it is Sam out of bed, her heart leaping, dumb animal, because it just *knows* those are his sleepy feet padding down the hall to her room. She knows those feet, the sound of them, their taste (when he was a baby she nibbled his toes to get him to giggle) and she rises to go to him. *Was it a bad dream? Is he sick?* She sits up in bed, is turning to put her feet on the floor, then remembers.

"What's the matter?" Dan asks, half-asleep.

"It's nothing."

The child isn't dead, he is only sleeping. She repeated those words to herself at the funeral, the words Jesus had said when he saw Jairus's dead daughter, because it was both easier and harder to believe that her son's soul was resting in God while his body slept in that little box, waiting to be wakened at the final resurrection, than it was to believe in the complete non-existence of Sam. How could Sam be gone? He was gone and she felt his goneness so palpably it was a millstone around her neck. *You killed your little boy.*

Today she will try not to dwell in those thoughts, this sunny afternoon with seeds in the ground and lines of poetry still lingering on her tongue. No. Today the house does not feel so barren. Today the house feels full of light and possibility and, well, if not Sam, then the fuzzy echoes of toppled blocks and tiny truck wheels. She once, in Kalispell, left him alone with a *Wishbone* episode only to return from the garden to find him gone. She remembers telling the story to Dan on the phone during his lunch break. She said, "I discovered today that our son enjoys wearing food." Dan laughed. "What do you mean?" And she told him how she'd followed a trail of tiny red handprints up the stairs, careful not to put her own hands in the globs of ketchup on the banister. How, when she reached the top of the stairs, Sam had leapt out and shouted, "I'm ketchup!" And he was wearing only ketchup. From the crown of his head to the tops of his feet the boy was covered. He looked up and gave her a gooey toddler giggle, and while he waited for her to respond he continued absentmindedly rubbing the ketchup into his shoulder and belly like sunscreen.

How had she responded? She'd screamed. She'd laughed. She'd pursed her lips. But as she ferried him giggling to the bathtub had she been grateful? There was no way she could have known what she'd had, you never do. She knew that now, but in the moment had there been some small glimmer? Some small voice that had said *seize this?* He had used half a bottle on himself—she knew because the bottle had been nearly full before he'd gotten his hands on it, and there is a poem somewhere in all this. She can feel it wanting to coalesce even as she feels herself wanting to withdraw. She forces herself to stay with it, to recall the now-bitter sound of Sam's laughter, to let it run through the house, to grab it with a phrase. She shifts her gaze from the ceiling to the page. Her eyes catch on the splayed book's back cover:

> *Eloquent and accessible,* Sprigs of Sun *is Paulette Kinchla at her best—a dazzling invitation to attend once again to the little revelations of the coastal Maine landscapes that have been at the heart of her verse for three decades.*

> *Whether she's bearing witness to the tumult of the seasons, conversing with native trees, or grieving the loss of Brady her beloved cocker spaniel—*

Grieving her *what? There is a poem in this!* a puny voice insists, but she feels foolish. The foolishness is crashing down on her like a wave. *Why should this new information discount*—those curls not the blond hair of a boy but the shag on the ass-end of a dog—it *does*. Her son is gone and will never come back and she can hear Dan (perfect timing) tromping though the back door. "Hello? I'm home! Hello?" His footsteps are heavy on the stairs, and then he is behind her. His arms wrap around her. Too loudly he says, "Baby, what's the matter?"

It was all so stupid, the ketchup, the poem, the dog who was not actually their son, and good god, if Dan doesn't already know what's the matter, he never will. The puny voice says, *Ask him to work with you in the garden.* But that isn't even an answer to his question. She pulls away from his arms. She wipes her eyes. "You wouldn't understand."

Here he comes, down the stairs, tinged pink from the shower and almost whistling. He isn't actually whistling, but his lips are set in a cheery pucker. He's decided to act as if the outburst last night never happened.

She takes a sip of her coffee and feels him looking her over. She knows what he's going to ask. He is desperate to worm them back into the false peace of the past two days. He looks down, deferential: "I know I just asked you last week, but I think you should think about it, driving again. It's a really beautiful morning."

He walks to the refrigerator to get the milk and does not wait for—or apparently expect—a reply. The milk jug is empty. He tosses it in the garbage, then reaches back into the fridge for the half-and-half and pours that on his cereal.

"I'll do it. Give me the keys."

"Really?"

"Yes."

He puts the keys on her *Missoulian* and then sits down, not across from her, but beside her. "Are you sure? You don't have to if you don't want to. I don't want to force you."

"It's something I need to do and today is as good a day as any."

"Okay."

For a second she thinks he is raising his hand for a high-five. He isn't, but he could've been. He is rising to retrieve his cereal. He doesn't want her to see how pleased he is.

She picks up the keys from the table. They are heavier than she remembered and warm from being in Dan's pants pocket. "I'm going to adjust the mirrors and the seat. Meet me in the garage when you're ready."

The air in the garage smells hazy brown, a mixture of grass clippings and gasoline, but the Subaru looks no more or less menacing than it did the day before.

Sitting in the driver's seat she finds the pedals too far from her feet, the steering wheel tilted down at that weird Dan angle, her heart beating just a little faster, but she does not feel overwhelmed. She'd thought maybe she would have a flashback or something, but she doesn't. She's been riding to work in this car every morning. She's just sitting in a different seat.

She pulls down the rearview mirror so she can see behind her, then adjusts the seat and the steering wheel and everything becomes familiar. She waits for the garage door to rise, then gently backs the car down the driveway. Dan taps on the window.

"Leaving without me?"

"Thinking about it."

Dan climbs in and buckles up.

She puts the car in drive, eases into the stop at the end of the road, and flips on the turn signal without even thinking about it. The mechanics have all come back. What is unnerving is the view out the windshield—cars rocketing down Orange Street, no gap between them, or at least none big enough to make her feel all right about pulling out, and now there are two cars backed up behind her, waiting. A gap comes. She shuts her eyes, not quite all the way, and makes the turn.

She opens her eyes. She drives under the railroad tracks, through the tunnel into town. Dan's hand has been on her thigh the whole time, a reassuring squeeze she resents for reasons she can't wholly articulate to herself at the moment. She glances down at his hand and he removes it.

She navigates the traffic with an ease that makes her feel foolishly proud of herself. She passes the courthouse and the bagel shop and the bars and stops at the light.

There are protestors camped out on the courthouse lawn again now that the weather's turned warm, and more of the same protestors across the street sipping coffee outside the bagel shop, their signs propped against the sidewalk tables. It is a protest where they seem to be advocating for everything. "Food, Not Bombs," says one sign, and another says, "Blue Skies and Coal Don't Mix." A third has a quote it attributes to Martin Luther King Jr.: "Our lives begin to end the day we become silent about the things that matter." The protestors seem happy to be out in the warm air.

The light changes and Sarah takes the Higgins Street Bridge across the river, a straight shot to the laundromat. She eases into the parking lot and leaves the motor running for Dan, who will take the car another mile south to the high school.

He comes around the front of the car, and she can see his eyes are full of love.

She says, "Don't ruin this by saying that you're proud of me."

He hesitates. "I wasn't going to say that."

"I love you," she says.

A clingy hug. He says, "I love you too."

iv. new loops

"**What routes do you** like to run?" she asks as she studies an ad for running socks in her magazine. "I used to run down by Fort Missoula, but now I'm living closer to the river and I'm trying to find some good loops."

"My goal is to run from my house to the foot of Mount Sentinel and back without stopping. I live over on the north side of the tracks. So far about all I can do is alternate running and walking to the dog park, but the walking is getting less. I'm making progress."

"That's great, Dan. You gotta keep it up."

"Thanks—sorry I don't know any loops for you."

She looks back down at her magazine. *Think,* he thinks, *think of something to say.* But nothing comes, and she turns the page. She turns another and then another, and then she puts the magazine in the basket with the others. She stands. "All right, I'm off. Have a good one, Dan."

"You too," he says, and he watches her go.

Throughout the afternoon, in his mind, he watches her go again and again as he replays their increasingly tepid interactions: *That's great, Dan. Keep it up. That's great. You'll get there. Take it easy. See ya later. Have a good one.* Two weeks have come and gone. It's mid-May and the world is warming and Carolyn Lakes is up the hall making photocopies.

He woke Saturday, the morning after he'd first seen her on the bridge, and considered not running at all, thus guaranteeing he wouldn't see or be tempted to search out Carolyn Lakes, but as he spat his toothpaste into the sink he found that his body wanted it, almost needed it, the running. How else could he face Sarah at the breakfast table?

So he ran across the Higgins Street Bridge and avoided the riverside trail altogether. He went past the bead store and the bistro and that overrated tapas place (such small portions) and ran almost all the way to Sarah's laundromat before turning right at the florist's into a more residential patch of streets. He did this Saturday and Sunday, and on Monday he was feeling good about his new route. He was putting distance between himself and those weird feelings about Carolyn Lakes. He was holding out for Sarah, *a little more time and she'll come around. Be patient. Slow and steady.*

Across the bridge, past the restaurants, right at the florist's—it was here that the thoughts drained from his mind and he began to hit a stride. His legs and his heart were pumping in accord, and he was making good time. His mind was blank like water but then—*oh shit!*—he saw her up ahead, Carolyn Lakes trotting down the porch steps of a townhouse, off for a jog in tight shorts and a sports bra, her midriff exposed.

He took a panicked right into an alley and nearly collided with the grille of a bread truck with its turn signal turned on. The driver jabbed the horn and Dan kept going. He did not look back. He was too embarrassed.

He assured himself as he headed back toward the river that Carolyn Lakes hadn't seen him—*but what if she had?* It was the natural thing to do, after all, to turn your head when a car horn sounded. Maybe she'd seen him, he thought as he showered, ate his cereal, and drove his wife to work. *But so what if she saw me?* he thought. It wasn't like he'd been looking for her—just the opposite. It was a coincidence and Carolyn Lakes wouldn't think anything of it—assuming, of course, she'd even seen him at all.

No, the real issue was something else entirely. He was feeling guilty for desiring the company of this woman who was not his wife. Deep down he knew that, he wasn't stupid, but fretting like a kid on a bike about whether or not Carolyn Lakes had seen him was so much easier than feeling lousy about the state of his marriage.

At lunch in the teachers' lounge that afternoon Carolyn looked up from *Runner's World* to ask him if he'd run that morning and how had it gone, and he couldn't help himself, he told her all about it, omitting only the part where he nearly ran past her house. He told her how much he liked running, how he'd never imagined he could like running. He did not tell her why he'd started running in the first place and she seemed to know not to ask. Instead she asked if he'd ever considered running a 5k, then suggested several upcoming races he might register for. He said he would think about it, and that after-noon, while his students got a start on their homework, he opened a new tab in his browser and began looking up races.

When he picked Sarah up from her shift at the cleaner's that evening she barely responded to his questions about her day. She stared—*blandly? coldly? angrily?*—out the windows as she delivered her one-word replies and just like that he felt angry, guilty, and defiantly not guilty all at once. He hit the turn signal with more force than was necessary and braked hard at each stop light, but if she registered his anger, she didn't show it. He lurched them to a halt at the light, and a flock of joggers came streaming through the crosswalk, a few shirtless men but mostly women in sunglasses and tight Nike apparel, and as he watched them file past his bumper a yoke lifted from his shoulders. *Why bind yourself to her misery?*

That evening he left her alone. They ate in silence, but he decided he didn't mind. In fact, he decided his silence was a gift. *It's what she's been wanting, dinner without chatter,* he thought as he speared a bit of pork chop. He felt all right, and he wasn't even thinking about Carolyn, not really.

He felt loose and light, happy even as he fell asleep, rose, ran, ate breakfast. He talked to Carolyn at lunch, and it was easier this time because he hadn't run into her that morning. He asked, "What 5ks would you recommend to a beginner?" and she said, "Get a pen."

Sarah came home late that evening without calling ahead to say so, but that didn't bother him, not really. She was an hour late, only a whole hour, but the soup was still warm. So, no harm done. A nosy pastor came by to check up on them, and when Dan chased him off he saw—saw it in her eyes—that he'd pleased her.

After that he didn't even have to decide that their dinner table silence was all right, it just was, and he began to realize it was a superpower, this new not caring. Carolyn Lakes was like gamma radiation—their little conversations unloosed something in him that now allowed him a certain latitude with Sarah. He could accept her as she was and wait patiently for her heart to heal as his had healed. By holding back he could draw her in.

That night, as he fell asleep staring at the shadows on the ceiling, he vowed again to win her back.

That was last Tuesday, twelve days ago. Today, Sunday, Sarah is two stone steps ahead of him on her way into the church, and she's as icy as the organ music. He reminds himself again that he has vowed not to give up. *Be chipper. Be cheerful. Slow and steady wins the race.* She leads him into an empty row near the back of the sanctuary, and he watches the walkers and O$_2$ tanks shuffle by. She is sitting a yard away from him in the pew. Who is he kidding? Sarah doesn't want him here. She doesn't want him at all.

The organist makes a key change and plays louder, and the little pastor parades in with the candles and the gold cross and the acolytes. He's as bald as Elmer Fudd, and his white robe drags behind him on the carpet, too big, like he's a kid dressed in his daddy's clothes, and as the service begins Dan forces himself to reflect on the past week's more promising developments. She's driving now, has driven him to work every day this week. That has to be good. The sight of her with her hands on the wheel, no trembling, all determination, it swells his heart, but he holds it in so as not to upset her. When she drives he wants to touch her, run his fingers through her hair, place his hand on her thigh, but he knows he ought not to. *Be patient, this is good.*

He rests his hand palm-up on the pew. Maybe she'll take it. Last week she put her head on his shoulder while they watched Mulder and Scully argue over what's possible, and he'd felt so aroused just holding her. But he held back, didn't push it. He sensed that something special, something fragile, might be unfolding, and he didn't want to blow it. He should have known she would be the one who'd ruin it, crying in the office, not interested in talking. She never wants to talk.

"Come now, let us settle the matter," reads the woman at the lectern. "Though your sins are like scarlet they shall be white as snow. . . ." She reads on, more readings, another hymn, and then the little pastor is shuffling to the pulpit. His voice is the singsong cadence of Kermit the Frog but slowed down to a dirge: "What we have hyeere is the laanguage of a laawsuite: 'Hyear me, you heavens! Listen earth, for the Looord has spoken: I reared children and brought them up, but they have reeeebelled against me. The ox knows its myaster, the donkey its own manger, but Is-rye-el does not know, my people do not understand."

The voice is easy to tune out, and it isn't long before the pastor has broken the bread and the ushers are nodding people forward to the altar rail for communion. Sarah goes forward without waiting for Dan. She knows that he won't and he doesn't. What's the point? He stays seated, head lowered, and thinks about his life. What a mess.

He does what he can (the dishes, for instance) and tries to be cheerful, and in the mornings he runs. Sometimes he sees Carolyn, but mostly he doesn't, and then at lunch they talk about stretches and running socks ("They're seriously worth investing in") and the articles she's been reading from the old magazines people have left in the corner basket. Interesting and innocuous and friendly enough, and then he goes home and Sarah is silent or moody or combative but never interested in talking about why. *But that's okay,* he tells himself, because he is being patient and life has begun to feel like something he can bear.

Something he can bear? As they file out of the church into the harsh light of noon he suddenly finds it hard to believe he has been even partially able to delude himself into thinking he felt happy. The more Sarah improves the worse she gets. Driving will solve nothing, gardening will solve nothing, the gift of his silence will solve nothing, and just like that, as they walk down the stone steps, it dawns on him all the ways Carolyn Lakes is like Sarah and all the ways she most definitely is not. Blond hair, sure, quick smiles, long legs. At first glance a similar appetite for books and for learning, but Carolyn sees surface where Sarah would see depth. She is too matter-of-fact in her outlook, too black-and-white, too young. Or is it that he has become too old? Either way the energy he expends looking forward to their encounters only leaves him feeling sad.

On Monday, without looking up, Carolyn says, "Have you signed up for any of those 5ks yet?"

"Not yet, but I will. It'll be good for me. I definitely will." He stands and gathers his papers. "Well, I'm gonna go get some problems on the board for my next class. Have a good one."

"You too, Dan. Have a good day," and she returns to the article she was reading.

He stops on the way home from school to fill the tank, and at the pump he accidentally opens his wallet upside down. Everything spills out—old receipts, spare change, two dollars, a ticket stub, credit cards, gift cards, punch cards, club cards, insurance information, a fortune cookie fortune, his license, and a photo. He squats down to gather them from the pavement.

He'd forgotten the photo was in there. He'd snatched it off the freezer when they were boxing up the pictures in the house and had tucked it in his wallet thinking he'd look at it every day at school before the students filed in. There was a white crease running through it now, down his cheek and his torso: he and Sam kneeling in the church gym where Sam's scout group still meets. Little cap, little ears, his mother's dark eyes. There's a derby car in his hands that they'd painted to look like a fire truck. They'd been beaten that day by a kid whose father was an engineer, but there are three smiles in the picture if Dan chooses to count Sarah, who was behind the camera. He can't remember the last time he's looked at this picture, has no memory of ever removing it from his wallet. Maybe he put it in and never took it out, not even once.

The pump clicks and he screws the gas cap back on. What he needs is someone to talk to, but who is there? There is no one. He and Sarah no longer have good friends who live close by, only colleagues from work and acquaintances they'd picked up at Peak Church, and the church people are no good. He and Sarah (this, at least, they have in common) find their pity and their platitudes insufferable. (Everything happens "for a reason.") Family's out too. Derek is too eager, his mother too full of concern, and his father will just ask him to come over and chop firewood. Sarah is the person he always went to with his problems.

He takes his phone from the cup holder and thumbs through his contacts. He could call one of his old friends from college, but he knows he will hold back, listen as his buddies speak about their jobs and their wives and their toddlers and then in return he will offer them a processed-packaged-freeze-dried update on his own life. "Hang in there," they'll say. "Hang in there, man."

He puts the phone back in the cupholder and pulls out of the gas station.

On the front porch, as he slides his key into the lock, he hears a man's voice in the living room, low and loud and verberating through the front door. It booms as he enters: "Go away! We don't want any!"

Derek laughs as he removes his boots from the coffee table. He draws Dan into a hug and says, "'Bout time you showed up—I need a refill." He presses a mug into Dan's hands, then pulls it away. "Just kidding, just kidding. Come in, sit down."

Derek throws a thumb over his shoulder at Sarah, who is looking partly sunny for once, seated sideways in her wingback chair, her legs draped over the arm, a mug cupped in her hands. "Your wife and I were just talking about my new position with the Forest Service. I was just saying you two gotta come visit. From the top of the tower it's mountains beyond mountains and the blue shadows of mountains in the distance, whole oceans of air filling up the valleys, most beautiful thing you ever saw, swear to God."

"And you left your post?"

"Figured it was high time I paid my good friend Sarah here a visit. Didn't realize you'd come barging in interrupting. And don't forget our refills—we're drinking chamomile. Just kidding. For God's sake, sit down! Take off your shoes!"

Dan lowers himself into the rocking chair like an old man.

"Enough about me," Derek says, angling away from Dan and back toward Sarah. "Are you writing? What have you been working on?"

She shakes her head. "Nothing worth reading. I've gotten a little out of practice."

"Out of PRACTICE?" Derek bangs his fist on the coffee table. "Well, damn it, then you've got to come to the tower. One look at the view and you'll *piss* poems. You'll piss poems and shit a novel."

"*Derek*," Dan says, but Sarah's smiling now.

"No, no," says Derek, rising again. "This woman is a *poet*, a—" he takes her hand and holds it up "—a goddamn bonafide professional published *poet*, and we can't have her depriving the world of her art and genius." He takes a deep breath and Dan knows what's next. Derek says: "'Winter, I swear, these bones have gone dormant, that hope is too warm a word—and yet there's the sun like Christ behind snowy clouds, a bright light visible for its veiling.'"

Derek raises his eyebrows at Dan as if to say, *Good shit, right?* The poem is one of Sarah's earliest, one she'd published on some blog of a magazine when she was still an under-graduate. It is perhaps the only poem Derek has ever read in his life. He memorized it as a welcome toast to Sarah on the Christmas Eve of Dan's proposal.

"That," says Derek, "is some artful verse. All right, what's for dinner?"

Dan looks over at Sarah—it's her night to cook—and she nods him back to Derek.

"That's right," says Derek, "elk chili, caught and cooked by yours truly. You two sit back while I go and dish it out of the crockpot. I'll find what I need."

As he hobbles to the kitchen Dan leans toward Sarah and says, so softly that he almost only mouths it, "Has he been *drinking?*"

"It's a show—he's baiting you and you always play right into his hand. He says he's given up alcohol."

"I've heard. How do we know he didn't come here straight from the Golden Rose?"

"Well for one you can smell it when he drinks. But he really did sound sincere when he was telling me about it. You should be happy for him. I'm happy for him."

You're never happy.

Over dinner Derek regales Sarah with firefighting stories, bar jokes, and embarrassing episodes from Dan's adolescence. He doesn't tell the stories so much as he performs them, with sweeping hand gestures and different voices for each character:

"It turned out he'd left the bathroom unlocked, so I just walked in and said, 'Dan, Jillian Baker's on the phone for you,' and dammit if he didn't jump out of the shower, buck naked, and put both his hands around my neck"—here he grips the upturned ladle with both hands and throttles it for emphasis—"so I dropped the phone and wrestled his hands from my larynx and hightailed it out of there, and, well, I don't remember. Dan, was she still on the line?"

"She'd hung up."

"Yeah, but you still took her to prom, so it was no big deal." He leans back in his chair, full of chili, and surveys the room. "You know, a new coat of paint might do this place some good."

Sarah nods. "We talked about that just the other week—we decided it'd be too much work."

"Might be worth it. A new coat of paint, some new house plants, a bigger TV—how do you not have a flat screen? Mom and Dad have a flat screen."

"What are you, an interior decorator?"

"No, but I could be, and God knows you need one. You have my number, right?"

Derek rises to clear the table, insisting very loudly that he be allowed to clear the table. Sarah drifts back to her blue chair. Dan follows his brother into the kitchen with the cloth napkins and water glasses.

"Just leave everything in the sink. I'll take care of it."

"Nah, I got it," he says, and he begins washing the bowls with a sponge.

"Fine. I'll dry."

Derek hugs Sarah and says goodbye. Then he nods for Dan to see him out.

On the porch Derek speaks in a lower voice: "She's not well. Mom's worried about you both. I know you'll come around, but I'm not sure she knows how to work out the poison. You two still seeing that grief counselor?"

"That's none of your business." (The answer is no.)

"It is my business, you shithead." He cuffs Dan on the back of the skull. "She's family, you made her family, and I think you ought to be taking better care of her. She's struggling bad. You can't see that?"

He shakes his head like he's disgusted and starts down the porch steps toward his truck, which he has somehow managed to park directly beneath the moon. He starts the engine, then leans over to unwind the passenger-side window. "Come and see me some time," he says. "And get your head out of your ass."

He rumbles the truck up the street, turns right, and disappears. The exhaust from the truck floats up toward the moon to merge with the air. Dan lingers on the porch.

When he heads back inside he finds that the house has grown quiet. Sarah's gone upstairs without him, and the living room has settled into a sigh, a sigh of relief at Derek's de-parture, but the stillness congeals as he climbs up the stairs to join Sarah in the bedroom. She is at the dresser removing her earrings. He comes up behind her to kiss her on the neck. He places his hands on her hips.

"So you think it might be a good idea to repaint the downstairs?"

"I don't know, Dan," she says, slipping away. "Can we talk about it tomorrow?"

"Why can't we talk about it tonight?" He is following her up the hall.

"I'm tired."

"So when Derek suggests painting the house it's worth considering, but when I suggest it, it's stupid."

"Yes, Dan. That's exactly correct." She passes him his toothbrush. She scrubs and she spits. "I never said it was a stupid idea. I just said I didn't feel like it."

"*Sebmankics*," he says as he works furiously on his molars.

"What?"

He spits. "Semantics."

"Well, if you want to paint, be my guest. Go down and start now. I'm tired. *I'm* going to bed."

"Maybe I will," he says as he follows her up the hall and into the bedroom. He snaps off the lamp and counts by thirteens until his jaw begins to unclench.

In the morning he vows again to swallow back his if-onlys. He runs, goes to work, skips lunch in the teachers' lounge. He has resolved, once again, to re-win his wife's affections—if Derek can make her smile, then *dammit*, so can he.

After work, on his way to pick up Sarah from the laundromat, he stops at the Safeway for a plastic-wrapped bouquet and then at the drive-through for two Hoagieville hot dogs, Sarah's guiltiest of pleasures back in their college days. The scent of carnations mingled with the smell of foil-wrapped chili cheese dogs, that's the smell of hope, the smell perhaps even of victory, so warm and thick it would have fogged the windows of the car on a cold day.

He parks and pushes through the double glass doors—both of them, like a gunslinger. Usually he waits in the car for Sarah to come out, but not today. Today he is New Dan, Big Dan, Dan Juan, Dan-victus. Carnations in hand he approaches the counter. The girl behind it is preparing to sew a button back onto a coat. Her tongue is poked out between her teeth. She is concentrating, jabbing at the eye of her needle with a bit of thread that won't go through. He says, "Hi, is Sarah back there finishing up?"

The girl looks up and smiles at the flowers. She gives him a wink. "I'll go get her for ya, Mr. McD."

A moment later Sarah emerges from the steam machines. Her eyes narrow on the flowers.

"Hi." He holds out the bouquet. She takes his arm and walks him out the door.

In the parking lot he presses the flowers against her and holds them there. She takes them and he turns to unlock the car. "Those are for you," he says as he jingles through his key ring. He opens her door with a sweep. "And that's not all!" Immediately he winces—he didn't mean to come off sounding like Big Top Dan, King of the Midway, but there it is: he's nervous. He shuts the door behind her and hurries around to the driver's side.

"I got us dinner!" he says.

"I noticed."

"Yeah!" That voice, he can hear it, why can't he stop it? His Meet-the-Mayor Voice is what Sarah used to call it. She used to tease him about it, pantomiming over-earnest handshakes as he spoke on the phone with potential employers, telemarketers, his mother.

She lays the flowers on the armrest and stares through the windshield.

"Do you like them?" he asks.

She takes a breath. "You don't have to do things like this, Dan."

"Well, I know I don't *have* to, but—"

"I mean, how is this supposed to make me feel? You should've given the flowers to Mandy. Flowers from a man,

Mandy would have burst. The look on her face when she came and got me." She makes a scoffing sound.

"Can't you just say thank you?"

"What?"

"Nothing. Nothing at all. I'm sorry I got you flowers."

The light turns yellow, and Dan eases them to a stop. Three bicyclists ride past single file in a low gear. Their feet churn and churn, but they move at a mosey.

"I'm such a bitch. I'm sorry, Dan. I mean it, I'm sorry. I just— It was a nice gesture. I'm sorry."

"Damn right."

"Dan, I still can't hear you. You're mumbling. Can you speak up? I'm sorry."

"I said I got your favorite. I stopped at Hoagieville."

"Thank you, Dan."

She takes the hotdog from the paper sack and peels off the foil. She takes two small bites, then wraps it back up. They drive on in silence past the ice cream place where he had planned on stopping, but ice cream no longer seems like a good idea. He can see the evening stretching out before them: back to the house, to the kitchen, and then back to the bed, more counting. As he drives he feels the narrative—*Couple loses son, couple falls apart*—hemming him in, cutting off his exits like a rook on a chessboard. *A clear head will find itself,* but who can help him clear his head? There is no one—not Sarah, not Derek, no one. Only Carolyn Lakes seems at ease around him, and that's because she mostly ignores him.

That night, in bed, after an evening of uneasy silence, he rolls over. He puts his arm around her, and she tenses. She says, "I'm not ready for this."

v. fig leaves and rags

She's driving him to work now almost every day. She drops him at the school before doubling back toward the laundromat or the house, and sometimes she cries. Sometimes she feels as if she is killing something and killing it again every morning. Other days she looks clear-eyed at the sun. Red-orange and cresting, it dissolves the clouds that float in the gap between the mountains. What she feels then is relief.

A new prayer has crept into her heart: "If you don't want me to, you should stop me." She paused one morning mid-psalm and said it: Let the God who placed the earth on a stand abandon her or intervene. But the Lord has yet to throw up any road-blocks and the driving gets easier every day. She suspects there is no whale coming to fetch her from Tarshish, that when she goes she will be gone, to soggy Oregon, to the Pacific, to some pale new life. Like Cain she'll wander the coast, rejected of God.

She will finish what her carelessness began—she feels sure of it when she watches Dan diminish in the rearview mirror. The leaving, once it starts, will be swift—which is maybe why she's still hesitating.

At the laundromat Mandy Merritt meets her eyes from behind the register: *Have you read them?* Sarah keeps walking. She pulls a skirt from the machine and begins gathering up the pleats to be pressed. As far as she can tell, Dan has no idea what's coming, no clue that every morning is a rehearsal, that she is working up the nerve. The Lord didn't stop her from stowing a duffle bag beneath the spare tire in the trunk.

Each time Dan buckles the passenger-side seatbelt he is filled with a fizzy, bottled-up pleasure, a gassy hope that will, no doubt, soon produce another belch of optimism. Flowers? Hot dogs? She wants no part of his hope. When he hugs her from across the armrest her muscles get tense. It's a small thing, but he feels it and a dark shadow passes across his face. He stuffs it down, smiles, says, "I love you."

"I love you too."

If she doesn't leave soon she will destroy him. She still kisses him on the stairs every morning, and she feels disgusted with herself every time. *Lord, you should stop me.*

But the Lord does nothing.

"Things are going badly," she admits when Bethany calls to see if the Kinchla book arrived.

"What do you mean?"

"You know what I mean."

"Okay, but you should still say it."

"Things are going badly."

Bethany sighs, and Sarah hears the clink of a spoon in a mug. She's stirring honey into her tea, would offer Sarah some if they weren't a time zone apart. She says, "Have you tried praying about it? Have you tried bringing your struggles to God?"

Sarah does not say yes. She takes a paper clip from her desk drawer and pings it into the waste can. She says, "I don't even know what prayer is anymore. Is it asking for things?"

"It can be."

"Then it's pointless. God doesn't give us what we ask for."

"What have you been asking for?"

"All night praying in the garden and what did Jesus get? He got crucified."

"Jesus was praying to know God's will, and to accept it."

"Exactly. The purpose of prayer is for God to blot us out."

She doesn't exactly believe that, but she says it anyway. She is feeling combative.

"If that's how you feel, you should tell God."

"Oh, trust me, God knows how I feel."

"But you need to say it. You need to *tell* him. If you do, you'll feel better."

"So prayer is really just about making ourselves feel good."

"*Sarah Schuller McDermott*, prayer is about entering the presence of the Lord your Maker."

She's toyed with her too much. After a moment she says, "How are the kids?"

"You're changing the subject."

"I am, but how are they?"

Nothing helps—what would help even look like? She wants to feel other than she does, but what other feelings are there? The feelings she has are the feelings she deserves. Nothing changes. She prays and God does not listen. She has not become more loving and Dan has not become easier to love. Small bugs are eating holes in the leaves of her plants as they emerge from the garden.

Then one morning, after dropping Dan off at school, she gets on the highway. It isn't a thing she planned on doing, but as she pushes the car up to 70 and merges she tells herself not to think too much about it. It's Wednesday, her odd day off in the middle of the week, and Dan won't miss her until after school lets out at 4 o'clock. *You don't have to decide what this means.*

She heads west and drives without music. She feels that God is not with her, but that he is trailing behind and above like a hawk. With the sun at her back she passes the airport and leaves Missoula. Tall grass and fence posts. She passes a colony of gas stations at Frenchtown, and then the ranchland gives way to the mountains and the trees become thicker.

She wavers a moment, glancing right for a pull-off to turn around, then she wills the car to go faster, 80, then 85. The river is weaving along beside her like an animal that is running, and the air is veiled with wildfire smoke. It thickens as she drives further west.

She passes a blue sign that says, "Welcome to Idaho," and with it a small sign announcing she's entered Pacific Standard Time. She pulls off at a gravel overlook and emerges from the car. She looks out across the ravine at the smoke-shrouded mountains. The tips of the trees are waving like tongues.

A tendril of breeze brushes by, a beckoning of air, and she looks down at all the trunks and outcroppings she would hit if she fell or stepped forward. Even so, she feels the urge, an impulse to step out into the open air, to cast herself off and declare something, to herself and to God also, who is still watching. If she wanted, she could do it. Right now. *You are worthless.*

She stares out into the air above the ravine and feels as if she is in two places at once, on the cliff and in the air, watching and falling, and it occurs to her that God will not stop her, that that is not how God chooses to operate. If she falls she will fall. Her life is like a stone in her hand. *I am alone.*

Just then a swell of wind at her back causes the branches to clamor. Behind her a twig cracks and she suddenly feels naked. She turns, sees no one. A semi whooshes by and rocks the car. She looks back at the ravine, the waving trees. Trembling, she fishes the keys from her pocket.

That night she wakes to the sound of Sam padding down the hallway. She sits up in bed, then remembers.

In the backwash of these moments she usually feels crushed. Tonight she feels anger. She drops her head to her pillow and knows she won't sleep. Here she is, awake in the dark, listening to the sound of train cars decoupling, and where is God?

I am here, says God, and she sighs. She shouldn't have brought him into it. Now that he is here he is going to hang around, lean on the dresser, wait for her response. She rolls over to ignore him but can't. She rises, careful not to wake Dan, and moves through the dark to the bathroom.

She shuts the door and switches on the fan. She closes the lid to the toilet and kneels down to pray. It occurs to her how foolish she must look, how if Dan came in behind her he might think she was throwing up. Maybe that's not so far from the truth. She recalls Bethany's words: *Tell God how you feel.* Instead she begins to pray the compline from memory, softly beneath the whir of the fan: "May the Lord Almighty grant me and those I love a peaceful night and a perfect end. Our help is in the name of the Lord, Maker of Heaven and Earth. Dear God, Almighty and Everlasting Father, I confess that I have sinned against you, through my own fault, in thought and word and—"

She feels God over her shoulder, shaking his head. *No, no. You know what to do*—God and Bethany in league with each other—but she won't. Instead she creeps up the hall, past Sam's room, to her office. She switches on the desk lamp and sets Mandy's poems in front of her like a foul-smelling meal. The poems God assigned her. *Here goes.* She unfolds the pages. She reads the first poem, rubs her temple, then sets it aside. She reads the second, then the third, then the fourth. They are bad, bad, bad—soppy angsty free verse, with words like "flooding" and "enveloped" and she keeps using "crimson" instead of "red." The poems are written in a heavy, accusatory second person toward a lover (or possibly, at times, toward a parent, hard to tell), with lines like "You push me like a bad magnet," "You toss me back and forth," and, somewhat promisingly, "You leave me cold on the plate."

She considers marking that last line, but doesn't. She reads on, deeper into the stack, noting and ignoring several good lines, and begins to feel disgusted with herself—it's the pity that needs to go, the poet's vacuous interest in overstating her own feelings, and Sarah is on to the Lord. She knows what he's up to, exposing her to such stuff. She's supposed to see that this is her, that she has become like these poems. She is the Israelites buried in dead quails, Hosea married to the prostitute, Ezekiel eating bread baked over human excrement.

There's nothing here worth keeping. She know this isn't true even as she thinks it. She sets the poems aside. She takes out her notebook and opens it to a page that's all-but-blank:

Dan,

She still can't figure out what should come next. The sentence that comes to mind is cliché, and the truth is not in it: *Dan, I love you and that's why I'm leaving. I'm leaving because I love you.* It's bullshit. Bullshit, bullshit, euphemistic bullshit.

You said it, not me, says the Lord.

Saturday night Dan goes out for drinks with the high school band director, Bobby Kemp. Dan was a trombonist in his youth and an on-and-off volunteer with the band boosters back when he was subbing at Sentinel and trying to get his foot in the door. He'd always gotten along with Bobby well enough, and it was easy to ask him to grab a drink.

He has rehearsed in his head what he wants to say, but he can tell that Bobby doesn't want to hear about Sarah. Bobby doesn't want to get within thirty feet of Dan's problems with Sarah. Instead he speculates about which of their stu-dents will make it into district band and district chorus. A gap enters the conversation and before Dan can speak, Bobby conjures another promising young trumpet player into the space. "A wonderful tone, Dan, the boy has a wonderful tone." He sets down his pilsner and dabs a bit of froth from his moustache. He says, "There's a musicality to his playing—you can hear him listening to the rest of the band as he plays."

Bobby is done after one beer, ready to return home to his wife and his cat. Dan slaps him on the back, "Don't worry about the tab, I got it," but when the waitress comes back and asks if he'd like another, Dan hears himself say, "Yeah, with some whiskey. A shot of whiskey. Please." He takes the shot first, throws it back, and clacks the glass down on the table. The whiskey makes him cough and sputter, and when he drinks the third beer he feels his face redden and warm.

After paying the tab he wanders out into the night, which is warm and alive with lights and colors. He walks up the block past the college bars, warm-lit places with clacking billiard balls and Dave Matthews on the jukebox. He follows the mingle of human voices spilling out the door, and when a space opens up at the bar he orders another drink, a whiskey Coke this time, and he drinks it fast. He is feeling reckless. He watches the pool players with their backwards hats putting away billiard balls with hard thrusts and incredible precision. He admires their confidence.

He notices a blond girl in tight jeans standing at the bar. He taps her on the shoulder and she turns, and he is surprised at how young she is. She has glitter on her cheeks.

"Can I buy you a drink?"

She frowns at him and he sees himself in her eyes: thirty years old with his polo shirt tucked into his jeans to mask his paunch, an orangey beard, a sweaty red forehead, Dan McDermott. The girl says no and turns back to the conversation she was having.

Dan drinks the ring of cola at the bottom of his glass. He sets the glass on the bar and turns to go. On the way out he bumps a pool player and ruins his shot. The kid yells something, but Dan does not look back. He slips out into the air and finds that the air has become cold. It's been a long time since he's had more than one. He is drunker than he thought he'd be—he discovers this as he walks—and in the cold air his thoughts turn bitter. He thinks of all the things God has stolen from him and he thinks of all the things Sarah has allowed God to steal from them and if there is no God then it is Sarah and Sarah alone who is to blame for the death of their son and the dissolution of their marriage.

It has never occurred to him before that the reason he has continued, in spite of himself, to believe in God is because he's needed God—not in any spiritual or emotional way, but because he's needed someone to blame, someone not Sarah. If he can't see Sarah as the victim of a callous God, then maybe he can't see Sarah as a victim at all. *I hate you,* he thinks suddenly.

A laughing couple brushes past him and releases a blast of music and chatter from the James Bar, and Dan finds himself in front of the quote he used to admire: *The tyranny of the rat race is not yet final.* What a fool he's been. How stupid. Look, it's a Hunter S. Thompson quote, and Hunter S. Thompson blew out his brains. His whole life he has been a fool and now, at thirty, his life is over. Sarah will never love him and neither will anyone else. He will never again find a person like Sarah, the old Sarah, and he will never again be a father.

He will tell her he wants a divorce. He will bang through the door and demand it. A di-*vorce*. He rolls the word around on his tongue like a club. She will weep and sob and apologize, and he will just shake his head, pack a bag, and then leave. Or they will embrace with ferocity and make love like they haven't in months. Months and months. He almost doesn't care which.

He walks past the bars and the shops through the tunnel under the railroad tracks back into his neighborhood. At the back door he takes a deep breath to let the anger pool into his lungs.

He is ready to storm in, but then he drunkenly fumbles the keys from his pockets and drops them in the shrubs.

Now he is down on his hands and knees rooting through the plants. He finds the keys and unlocks the door, and when he opens it he finds that Sarah has turned out the lights and gone to bed.

He hesitates for a moment and then wishes he hadn't. It is one thing to come home to Sarah at the kitchen table eating leftovers and to start bellowing. It is another thing entirely to wake her from a dead sleep and ask for a divorce he doesn't even want. For a while he just stands there with the door open with his feet on the mat.

Finally he begins to make his way through the darkened living room toward the stairs where Sarah left on a light, moving as quietly as his oafish body will allow, bumping an end table and wobbling a lamp before he starts up the stairs.

Halfway up he hears something and pauses: a thin trembling voice, Sarah's voice, but he can't make out what she's saying. Is she on the phone? He proceeds slowly and the contours of her voice come into focus. Her voice is trembling with anger. It is full of poison and spit and falls heavily on the word *you*.

"*You* are to be praised, O God, in Zion.

"To *you* shall vows be performed in Jerusalem.

"To *you* who hears prayers will all flesh come, because of their transgressions."

In his mind Dan can see her kneeling beside the bed with her elbows propped on the mattress, a prayer book spread open before her, her eyes bearing down on the words. They used to prayer together like that, on their knees, when they were first married, and it had seemed like such an intimate thing, a kind of nakedness almost, to join hands and kneel before God Almighty, except back then Sarah had never prayed with such—his liquored brain searches for the right word—such contempt. Her voice is full of contempt. She is praying like she's cursing. Can it be that she has come to hate God even more than he has? But it isn't that, not exactly, not with the words she is saying. It's desperation or self-loathing or—he can't think what. He listens.

"Our sins are stronger than we are, but you will blot them out. Awesome things will you show us in your righteousness, O God of our salvation, O Hope of all the ends of the earth and of seas that are far away."

She pauses, then begins a sharp new prayer:

"O Lamb of God who takes away the sins of the world, have mercy on us. O Lamb of God who takes away the sins of the world, have mercy on us. O Lamb of God who takes way the sins of the world, grant us your peace."

He won't go in until she is finished with the prayers. He will wait. But then he hears her flip a page and begin again, and he thinks perhaps she will do this over and over until he interrupts her.

He holds his head in his hands. His bluster is gone, he feels almost nothing, not even the chasm of if-only. He tries to stir up the old feelings of frustration, tries to hold them together and harden them so that he might form a fist with his heart and walk in, but he only feels empty, and now he feels a sudden pull toward prayer—he could walk softly through the door, kneel beside her like the old days, but the thought of opening the door, of turning the knob and walking through, it seems like too big a thing. He imagines Sarah pausing mid-prayer to look back at him, and he sees his own nothingness reflected in her eyes, and he knows he will find no words within him.

He turns and walks softly down the stairs to the couch.

'Kay was blue, almost black from the cold, but he didn't notice because the Snow Queen had kissed the shivers right out of him and his heart was a lump of ice. He kept arranging shards of ice in every way possible, trying to make something out of them—'

Daddy?

Yes, Sam?

Daddy, have you ever been associated with nose picking?

No, I have not. Are you associated with nose picking?

Sometimes.

Well you shouldn't— Don't *do that, Sam.*

Why not?

Because it's gross. Your mom and I don't like it, and your teacher won't like it, and the girls at pre-school definitely won't like it.

Girls *are gross, Dad.*

Before you know it you'll be in first grade and you'll be wanting to find a nice girl and settle down, get married, love her forever—but you won't be able to if you're associated with nose picking.

I'm never getting married.

I guess we'll have to wait and see.

(beat)

Could I marry Mom?

No, I'm afraid your mom is already spoken for.

What does spoken for mean?

It means she's already married. She's married to me.

Oh. Then I'm never getting married.

We'll see. Should we keep going? Can you turn the page?

(nods, yawns, turns the page)

'He put the ice shards together to form words, but he never could get the word that he wanted—that word was "forever." The Snow Queen had said, "If you find me that pattern . . ."'

She finds him on the couch, asleep in his clothes. His forearm is draped across his face like a paw to keep out the sun. He smells like an ashtray.

Under other circumstances she might have felt alarm, concern, anger, something, but this morning, seeing Dan passed out on the couch, she only feels exhausted. She takes the quilt from the rocking chair and lays it across him. His feet stick out because the quilt is too short.

She puts a mug of water in the microwave and while it spins she rummages through the pantry for instant coffee. She stirs in the crystals, sits down, and studies him from the kitchen table, his blond eyelashes, his freckled cheeks, the holes in his socks. There's a small crescent at each heel and a big one where the ball of his right foot has worn through. He looks, if not peaceful, then at least very unconscious, and when he does wake up he will wake to a monstrous hangover. Pain, pain, pain. No doubt about that. Her husband is not a studied drinker. The only time he's come home drunk were those nights early in their marriage when they came home drunk together and stumbled up the stairs to the bedroom, shedding shoes and belts as they went.

When she finishes her coffee she takes a glass from the cupboard and fills it high with water. She takes the Tylenol from the medicine cabinet and shakes two tablets into her palm. She sets them with the water on the end table above his head. She looks him over one last time, the soft skin through the holes in his socks, his face buried in the pit of his elbow, her husband sleeping like a child. She turns to go, then turns back. She sets the pill bottle on the end table beside the loose Tylenols and the water. Two will not be enough.

At church the pastor preaches grace, God slow to anger and abounding in love, sin separated from sinners as far as the east is from the west, compassion measuring from the surface of the earth to the roofbeams of the sky, and she sits there and she takes it, like a tree in the wind. "We feel vulnerable because we are vulnerable," the little pastor declares.

This morning the old man is—in his own slow scholarly way—full of fire. The stained glass behind him is ablaze with sunlight and behind the panes the shadows of tree branches bob and sway like rumors of another world. He says, "Luther taught that the Christian life is nothing other than a daily return to baptism, once begun and ever to be continued. He said we must clothe ourselves in baptism, that we must esteem it as our daily dress." He is speaking about the Festival of Booths, he reads somberly from Isaiah: "'Then the Lord will create over all of Mount Zion and over those who assemble there a cloud of smoke and a shade from the heat of the day, a refuge and a hiding place from the storm.'" And he says, "Just as the Lord covered the nakedness and shame of the first man and the first woman with animal skins he himself had sewn, so have you been covered in Christ's love and grace. Truly I tell you, just as the father took the prodigal son into his arms and placed his own robe upon the boy's shoulders, just so have you been clothed in Christ. Idolatry is when we seek cover from things that are insufficient, from fig leaves and rags." He says, "Nothing is sufficient but Christ."

Sitting in the pew she does and does not believe it, feels she ought to but cannot. His yoke is easy and his burden light, so light you can't feel it on your shoulders. She opens her notebook and reads what she wrote the day prior:

> *This is how you know. You have stopped biting the heads off animal crackers. You realize it at your desk one morning as you study its faux grain: Once you did and now you don't. You used to believe that this was the humane thing to do, but now you detrunk the elephants and maim all the llamas before you gnash them into paste, and what's more—be honest—you relish it. You linger too long on the railroad tracks. You drink deep breaths of cold morning air not for the air but for the sting. Like a bully you take Christ's cross for yourself, Christ who cried "Eloi, Eloi, lama sabachthani!" but the llamas are all maimed and won't answer, and the wafer has no legs and no head. The wafer is all one thing and it does not sting when it is placed on your tongue. The grape juice does not burn as it slides down your throat.*

Beneath the entry, as the preacher preaches on, she writes, *There is a place where the face of your son still lives, and this is the one place you won't go. In the end even your grief is hollowed out and taken from you.*

When she goes forward for communion she feels a childish impulse to seize the chalice from the altar server and pour it on herself. *Why can't God's truth be literal?* She could be like a woman in a shampoo commercial, wine running through her hair. Instead she dips her wafer in the cup like a good Lutheran and receives.

She sits down in her pew, bows her head, and tries to hold the taste of the wine on her tongue as she prays. When the congregation stands to sing the final hymn she slips out the back, a brisk walk out the door and down the steps. She wonders what she'll say to him when she finds him awake.

The air is bitter-dry as she starts her walk home from church, and there's no question about it anymore, taste and see: the smoke is blowing in from Idaho. But even in the haze the Clark Fork River is flashing with sun, and she recalls how she used to walk along the river imagining herself underwater. The Missoula Valley was once at the bottom of a glacial lake and she liked to imagine her footsteps stirring up ancient sediment.

She could sustain the illusion for herself as long as she looked at the river and not at the mountains. They were so much taller than the green hills back home, and she just couldn't imagine enough water to turn those ridges into shorelines. The lines were still there on the mountainside where the surface of the water had once been, but the lines somehow made it harder, not easier, to believe in the water.

She unlocks the back door and enters the kitchen, a Pine-Sol smell, and it's dark as a cave. *Is he here?* The couch is now empty. The quilt has been folded up as neatly as Christ's shroud and draped in its place on the rocking chair's arm. The mug and spoon she left on the counter are now in the drying rack beside the water glass she'd left him. A drip from the faucet hits the metal basin of the sink.

"Dan, are you here?"

She casts her keys onto the table, unshoulders her purse, and hears no response, no rinse of water from the shower upstairs, nothing.

She pops off her shoes and moves through the living room to the stairs, calls his name again, and heads up. Upstairs the bed is made. She'd left it rumpled, has never been great about bed-making, but now the duvet is smoothed out. The pillows have been sculpted into an aesthetic little mountain against the headboard.

"Dan, where are you? Are you here?" she says again, and then she sees it, a note taped to the bedroom window.

vi. actions and powers

He rounds a sharp turn, a switchback on a sloped gravel road, and the trees part like curtains to reveal mountains, mountains beyond mountains and the blue shadows of mountains in the distance, the decadence of God, and after he glances over he keeps his eyes set forward. Looking at the mountains is like tonguing something bitter that's caught in his teeth.

When he taped the note to the window he felt nothing, *it is finished*, not peace, not resignation, not rage, just nothing—no, not nothing, pain. He woke to the sun falling like an axe between his eyes, his neck kinked against the armrest of the couch, and the house was empty. She'd gone to church, had left him, had chosen something else.

Well *vaya con dios*.

He started to sit up but his stomach slugged to the side and made a swallowing sound. He squeezed his eyes shut and lay very still. His stomach gurgled again. He broke into a sweat. A loud lurch.

He started to his feet but was tangled in the quilt, and he shin-banged the beveled edge of the coffee table. He felt bile rising in his throat. He couldn't gulp it back and he wasn't fast enough to the bathroom. He spewed on the kitchen tile, a rank splatter. He straightened up to catch his breath, then splattered again.

He waited a moment and then another moment. *Okay.* He wiped his mouth with his shirt sleeve and felt lighter. He left the mess and went upstairs to the bathroom, tossed his shirt into the tub and rinsed twice with mouthwash. He could feel his stomach settling in, as if for a nap, as he scrubbed his teeth and tongue. He spat, then tossed the toothbrush into the trash.

He pulled on a t-shirt and headed downstairs to mop up his fluids with some old towels. His stomach murmured as he knelt to clean the mess, and he realized his head had been throbbing for a long time. The towels went straight into the trash. He tied off the bag and stashed it in the can out back. He knew he should mop, but first Tylenol and maybe a shower. He rummaged through the medicine cabinet, knocking q-tips and cotton balls into the sink. No Tylenol. *Where is it? It should be here.* The Tylenol was on the end table in the living room with a glass of water. He hadn't noticed it before, a little *fuck you* from Sarah. Whatever. He took the pills.

He showered with the lights turned out and let the hot shower water beat against his forehead. So much better. He dried off, then mopped the kitchen floor with Pine-Sol and peroxide, and as he passed the sponge across the tiles he felt as though he were erasing himself from the house. He folded the quilt, made the bed upstairs, then came down and did all the dishes in the sink. He sat down at the kitchen table and wrote a simple note that would let Sarah know where they stood.

That was his morning. After he taped the note to the window, he drove to the downtown hotels and passed them one by one, the Days Inn, the Doubletree, the Thunderbird Motel. He kept picturing the carpeting in the rooms, the bedspread, the nightstand. That rubbery just-vacuumed smell. He kept driving and found himself merging onto 90 East, and he knew then that he was driving to Helena and beyond Helena to the fire tower where Derek was stationed. He dialed the automated SubFinder system to called out sick for tomorrow, then powered down his cell phone so Sarah wouldn't be able to reach him.

He drove fast, the needle licking 90, and thought of nothing except the stabbing pain behind his eyes. Why hadn't he grabbed sunglasses? He saw a sign for a Conoco at the exit in Clinton but kept going. He felt that to stop and to stop so soon would prove fatal. He couldn't say what, but he knew he was outrunning something, or trying to. *Keep going.*

Somewhere around Drummond the Tylenol finally began to dull his pain, and that was when he began to blame her for what he'd done. *How can I be there for her if she won't be there for me?* He repeated variations of this thought over and over until he felt worn down by the highway driving and could no longer sustain his anger.

He stopped for gas outside of Garrison and then, with the town behind him, feeling tired, he wept openly, thinking *never, never again will you be a father.*

He was spent, shelled-out numb, when he left the highway outside Helena and found the gravel road that would take him to the tower, where the pine trees keep parting and embracing in the wind.

Now he rounds the final turn. The road ends at a clearing where he sees his brother's truck parked between a cabin and the base of the tower, and Derek is already hobbling down the steps to greet him. He must have seen him as a dust cloud from far off and recognized the Subaru.

Dan steps out of the car and allows Derek to pull him into a one-armed, closed-fisted hug. He is wearing rough yellow overalls, and the earthy smell of sweat wafts from its folds. He is in high spirits. He ruffles Dan's hair.

"You should've called!" He thumps Dan on the back. "I would've showered. It's good to see you. How you been?"

"I've been better."

"Well, we'll remedy that. I'll give you a tour."

Classic Derek, he does not ask what brings Dan all the way out here, and Dan is left to wonder what his brother has assumed as he follows him up the hewn wood steps.

"Eighty steps from the bottom to the top," he is saying. "The cabin there stands six thousand one hundred feet above sea level. At the top of the tower we'll be sixty feet above that. It's a hell of a view."

They pass through a wooden hatch into the windowed room at the top of the tower. Derek heaves the trapdoor shut behind them, sealing out the wind, and they are alone. Beyond them, below, the tops of pines are whipping in the breeze. Birds are suspended in the air, wings motionless as they circle some dead thing in the valley below. His marriage perhaps.

"Don't mind the mess," Derek says as he shuffles around the large brass fire finder in the center of the room. He closes his toolbox and sits down on top of it, motioning for Dan to take the wooden chair. "You see those little glass coasters under the legs? They insulate it from lightning strikes. Safest spot in the whole tower. You thirsty?"

Without waiting for an answer he reaches into a little cooler and tosses Dan a can of beer. Dan frowns as Derek opens a second for himself. Derek notices and grins.

"O'Doul's," he says, "non-alcoholic. Don't drink it too fast or it'll just leave you feeling disappointed." He takes a sip and sets the beer on the floor between his boots. When Dan says nothing, he reaches around into a box for a deck of cards and begins shuffling. He says, "It's a pretty good gig up here so far. Once an hour, from dawn to dusk, I scan the horizon and radio in an all clear to the fire desk. Other than that I can pretty much do as I please. They'll send a guy up to relieve me every other weekend, once the season officially gets started."

"That's it?"

"Well, if I was to spot a fire it'd get a little more involved, but yeah. Not much, but I like it. I've been keeping busy."

He squares the deck and begins dealing a hand of rummy. He stomps his boot against the floorboards.

"Last week I refinished the floor and built those shelves behind you. I've been improving the cabin too. My next project—as soon as I can figure out how to do it—is to clean the outside of these windows."

"I could hold your ankles."

"My brother the funny one. Take your turn."

They begin to play, and Derek continues talking, and for once it's nice to listen to him gab. It's nice not to have to think about what to say. What Derek talks about is the stars. He says there are bunks down in the cabin, but sometimes he sleeps in the tower just because he can. Because of the stars. He is learning to identify constellations from a book. While Dan shuffles Derek tunes the radio to a classical station and then apologizes, saying, "I know this is gonna make me sound like a dick, but I'm gonna say it: I think it's the only music that does justice to the view." This is almost more than Dan can take, but Derek starts talking about the stars again, regretting that Dan won't be able to see much, too much smoke in the air from "that mess" in Idaho.

Dan sips his drink and plays his hand, and he's wondering again why he came. The angry words he repeated to himself on the drive, they will only sound thin and whiny up here in the tower, with the mountains at their feet and goddamn Bach on the radio. *How can I be there for her if she won't be there for me?* he'd say, and the mountains themselves would respond: *Like you're the only one with problems.*

So, what then? Why had he come? To confess his sins? To Derek? If so, what is he to say? That he occasionally chats about running socks with an attractive young social studies teacher? What are his sins compared to Sarah's—and why does he suddenly feel responsible for those as well? He thinks of her, really thinks of her, for the first time since he left the note. By now she's found it. It's too late to take it back. He feels in his bones that she will leave him and leave him for good, and he is afraid to speak the premonition aloud, especially here, where everything is so quiet.

Derek breaks the silence: "When the settlement money from the accident comes in, I'm buying a sailboat."

"A what?"

"I've been reading about it," he says. "I'm going to sail

around the world—around the coast of the world. Stop at every port there is, stay as long as I want, see everything. The way I figure it, I'll have enough money and enough coast to last me five years if I do it right. I'm flying east in October to look at a boat, and I've signed up for sailing lessons in Jamaica this winter."

"Derek, you could buy a house. You could invest and live off the interest. You can't just spend that sort of money on a whim."

"I like the stars, I like the wind, I like my non-alcoholic beer. I'm not going back to Missoula this winter." He takes a drink. "Anyway, I wasn't asking your permission. I was making an invitation. You and Sarah should come with me this winter, down to Jamaica."

"There might not be a me and Sarah this winter."

"Oh, bullshit. You two just need to screw. Any day now it's bound to happen—I just hope it's not in a public place."

"It's not bullshit, Derek."

"It is bullshit," he says, and he becomes taller. "Look, just cause she tossed you out—"

"That's not what happened."

"—just cause she tossed you out doesn't mean—"

"That's *not*—"

"—*doesn't* mean that you—"

"That's *not* what happened! *I* left *her*."

"Pardon?"

"I left her."

"Fuck you, man." He throws his beer at Dan. The can is three-quarters empty and only splashes. He says, "What the fuck."

"You don't—" *Well, damn it, here I go.* He takes a breath. "How can I be there for her if she won't let me? How do you do that? She barely even looks at me anymore. She doesn't want anything to do with me."

"Fuck that."

"It's true. She doesn't even look at me, not in the morning and not at night. At dinner she snaps at me."

"Yeah, and she's one sorry-ass driver."

Dan springs to his feet. "*You*— You can shut the hell up."

Derek looks up at him and rubs his chin. "You want to take a swing at me?"

"No."

"Go ahead. Do it." He nudges out his chin.

"Shut up."

"Well what do you want from me? Why are you here?" He sits down. "I don't know."

"Well maybe you should go home."

"It's not my home anymore."

"Good god, you are a self-centered S.O.B." Derek's radio begins to crackle and he holds up a finger to pause the conversation. "I need to take this. Here," he lifts open the trap door, "go sit on the steps and cool the fuck down. Look at some nature or something."

Dan clenches his jaw but obeys. He climbs back through the hatch. Derek heaves the trapdoor shut behind him.

Sitting on the steps he looks out at the sun through the smoke, a red smudge on the horizon, not setting so much as it is just burning out, and suddenly all he can think about is how much he wants his wife, her lips, her arms, her hair, her body. He misses the warmth of her body.

He closes his eyes. When was the last time he felt happy? Really *happy?* He thinks of the blank white walls in their house, the little nail holes where the pictures once hung, and he remembers how they chose not to celebrate Christmas, not even in private.

But it had snowed on Christmas Day, big, thick flakes falling like moths, they blotted out the world, reduced parked cars and bushes to smooth white humps, and even the sound of the cars, the few that were out, was dampened, reduced to tires rubbering by, and Dan had been surprised to find himself regretting their decision not to observe the holiday, even though he was the one who'd suggested they skip it.

No gifts this year, but still the snow came down. He left Sarah curled in bed with a book—she wasn't interested in going out—and he pulled on boots and gloves and an old scarf he hadn't worn since college. He shuffled down the uncleared sidewalks past the closed shops and around to the lot by the railyard, which was empty, a blank canvas save for the iron rails, and the snow was still falling. He thought how Sam would have loved it, how his eyes would have looked, and somehow it was a hurting that felt okay.

When he got home, he stripped off his wet clothes and went upstairs to look in on Sarah. He was almost overcome by the desire to hold her tight in his arms, to tell her they were going to be all right, that the hurting would never stop but eventually the hurting would be okay. He knew, he had felt it. But she was already asleep with the pillow clutched to her face to keep out the light, and the sight of her made him unaccountably sad.

He took the book splayed open beside her on the mattress and placed it on the nightstand so she wouldn't lose her place. Then he walked downstairs and cycled restlessly through the options on the TV. He settled on the Yule Log, then stretched out and fell asleep in its false glow.

Sitting on the steps of the tower he opens his eyes. He tries to put it all out of his mind, the thoughts, the anger, every-thing, thinks nothing. He thinks suddenly of the way you gasp for air when you're plunged into cold lake water.

The wind dies down, the tree tops hold still.

For dinner Derek heats an open can of Nalley's chili on the propane stove in the cabin, then dumps the contents into a half-dozen flour tortillas and tops them with some shredded cheese from a bag and a few glops of hot sauce. There are, Dan notices, many cans of chili, baked beans, and Spaghetti-Os in the cupboard above the stove. In the bookcase by the door is a surprising mixture of star charts, sailing manuals, and used books with blue stickers: *The Old Man and the Sea, The Assassination of Jesse James, Cathedral and Other Stories, Leaves of Grass, Jesus Calling,* and *A Beginner's Guide to Buddhism.* He follows Derek out to the porch, and they eat with their feet propped on the wood railing, looking out at the dark spaces between the trees.

"**You once told me,**" says Derek, "that the *Christian* view, which is *Dan's* view, is that love is not a feeling, but a decision, an action, a deliberate choosing not to be selfish—do you remember this? This was back in college when you were in that cult. You said that when the Bible says God is love it doesn't mean that God is a warm feeling like piss in a pool."

"That's—"

"I'm paraphrasing. Bear with me. You said that God is like an action, an engine that gives off the universe the way other engines give off heat. I suspect you were cribbing Sarah, we both know she's the brains, but when I recall those words, which I do sometimes, I hear them in your voice. Do you remember?"

He remembers. It was Thanksgiving break junior year, a year into dating Sarah, and over beers at a sports bar he'd stumbled into talking about love as the unity of the Trinity. It was something he'd read about in one of Sarah's books, Thomas Merton: "Infinite sharing is the law of God's inner life." How anyone could ever, with confidence, write such a frank declarative sentence about God's inner life was beyond him, but the idea had found footing in his brain now that he had all these questions about engagement rings.

If love was nothing more than a feeling then he was shackled to chance and damned by statistics and doomed to fail her. But if, on the other hand, love was an active commitment, a choice he could make anew every morning, then with God's help he could love her every day and forever. He wanted advice from Derek, who was himself engaged at the time and knew about how much one should spend on a ring, but Derek only wanted to talk about God: "Tell me about that cult you're in."

So Dan told him about the people he'd met through the Christian campus group he'd gotten involved in, how some of those people had found Jesus' love so powerful and compelling they converted and got baptized, like Sarah. He explained that love and sin were kind of similar, when you think about it, at least in so far as both are not only actions but powers at work in the world that you could get caught up in, and love is the stronger force, the force that will win because it comes from God.

He'd once heard a pastor say that the love between God the Father and God the Son was so strong it gave rise to the third Person in the Trinity. Sarah had told him this wasn't quite accurate and was maybe heretical. She'd had a term for it, but she said it with a shrug. "There's almost no way to imagine the Trinity without being at least a little bit heretical—it's just beyond us." But for a while the concept had made sense: Dan loved Sarah and Sarah loved Dan, and their love was so strong it became a person and it was Sam.

"**I bring all that** up," Derek says as he picks a bean off his overalls and pops it into his mouth, "because I think you're pissing in the pool. No, let me talk. You're pissing in the pool and you shouldn't do that. I mean, she's your wife, right? For richer or poorer, sick or healthy, so help you God."

"Till death do us part."

"You're misinterpreting that line. What you gotta do is go home and beg her to forgive you. That's the only train running. And maybe she does and maybe she doesn't, but you gotta ask. I mean, this is pretty black-and-white. I'm surprised you had to drive all the way out here to hear it from me of all people."

After a moment Derek rises to carry their plates inside, leaving Dan alone on the porch, watching the tree trunks merge with their shadows as the night begins to thicken.

vii. defeat

She is straightening the spines of the books on the shelves, she is picking bits of fuzz off the carpet with her fingers.

She drags a kitchen chair into the living room and stands on it to wipe the thick grey dust from the fan blades with a wet paper towel. The loose dust hangs in the air like God and vice versa. She is waiting.

Yesterday, when she found the note taped to the window, she'd laughed. She did. He'd found the words she couldn't: *Maybe we're kidding ourselves.*

Maybe we are. She sat down on the corner of the bed and laughed into the palms of her hands, and, sure, it was a laughter like the sound of fabric tearing, but after she blew her nose she felt better. She thought it's all in the past tense now. She went for a walk by the river and took a long cliché look at the water under the bridge, and she decided that every time she'd said "I love you" she'd meant it, if not fully in the moment, then here now, on the bridge, in retrospect she meant each one fully and completely. For dinner she ate half a cheese pizza.

But today—how she hates him. He is coming back.

She woke up feeling fine, stretched her legs out into his side of the bed and called in sick to work. She skipped her prayers and poured cream in her coffee, feeling great, but then she felt a tug of concern and she had to go play detective.

On the computer she pulled up his credit card charges, a stop for gas in Garrison, so he'd either gone to his parents in Butte or to his brother in Helena. She called his brother.

"Sorry, Mario, your princess is in another castle."

"He's not with you?"

"He was with me, got here yesterday, but I sent him back to you."

"He's coming back today?"

"Oh yeah. I set him straight."

"When did he leave?"

"I said to him, you're pissing in the pool. I said, what you gotta do is beg her to forgive you."

"Derek, when did he leave?"

"I reckon about eleven-thirty. I made him eat breakfast before he left. Listen, go easy on him, but kick his ass, you know?"

Mental math: he was forty, maybe fifty minutes out.

She said, "Okay, well, thanks."

"Anytime. Don't do anything I wouldn't do."

She snapped the phone shut. "Well shit."

Now she is anger-cleaning the downstairs toilet, scrubbing with clenched teeth. What bothers her isn't so much that he left and is coming back as it is, well, you can't have it both ways. Stay gone and be forgiven or come back and say nothing.

She does not want to hold him and make him feel better about himself while he grovels.

What she should do is barricade the front door with the sofa, scatter thumb tacks in the foyer, tie a paint can to a string like Macaulay Culkin in *Home Alone*. Because she will not be foist into the role of Penelope, patient damsel—no, she will wound him, remind him who it is he is asking to forgive him. She gives the toilet an aggressive flush, then washes her hands and has an idea.

She removes the big flat box from underneath Sam's bed, and she carries it to their bedroom. She unweaves the cardboard flaps and dumps the old photos onto the duvet: birthdays, vacations, Christmases, the photo from the hospital on the day he was born, Sam like a beet pulled from the earth and laid on her chest.

And then, of course, a knock.

Fuck. She steps back to catch her breath and suddenly changes her mind. She tosses the pictures back into the box and shoves it underneath the bed. She looks at the ceiling. "Lord, I am tired. I don't know what you want from me."

The knocks come again, two iambs of knocking, KNOCK KNOCK, KNOCK KNOCK, a Dan rhythm, and the Lord says, "You should go get the door. Someone's here."

She goes down stairs, opens the door, and there he is, standing up straight on the porch, not so hang-dogged as she would've guessed, though his eyes do glance away from her face.

He shifts his weight from one foot to the other. "Hi."

An awkward pause.

Finally she says, "Do you want to come in?"

"Okay."

He stands in the living room with his shoes on and his hands in his pockets. He looks around the room at the furniture. It is as if he has entered a museum.

He turns to look at her, and he looks her in the eye. Clearly it's a speech he's been rehearsing in the car: "Sarah, I have been acting like a child—"

She throws up a hand. "I forgive you."

"I—" He frowns.

"It doesn't matter. I forgive you."

"Well I have more to say."

"No, really, I forgive you. Let's drop it."

Another awkward pause.

He says, "So what do we do now?"

She hadn't thought about that. She thinks of the photos beneath the bed. "I don't know. Don't you have some quizzes grade?"

"Sarah, it's not a small thing that I did."

She says nothing.

He says, "Let's go for a walk. Let's get a drink. What do you say?"

She can think of no counter suggestions. She puts on her shoes.

She keeps her hands in her pockets as she walks and says nothing. Beside her he exudes a pearly silence. In spite of the smoke it's a beautiful afternoon. People are everywhere, walking dogs, riding bikes, chatting across plots in the community garden.

At the restaurant he orders a grilled chicken salad and an amber beer and eats with a strong appetite. She shifts her tater tots around on the plate, avoiding his eyes. She watches the hockey game on the TV in the corner and drinks her beer too quickly. He drinks his slowly, in large intermittent sips, and focuses on the salad, spearing fronds of lettuce and swirling them around in ranch dressing.

"I don't know what you want from me," she says finally.

He pats his mouth with a paper napkin. He says, "I want to talk."

"Okay."

"I mean, do you want a divorce? Is that where we're headed? Because that's not what I want. I shouldn't have written that note, and I shouldn't have left like I did. I'm—"

The waitress is hovering at their booth. "Can I get you folks some refills?" She slops ice water out of the pitcher and into their glasses and squints to make a mental note of where they're at with their beers. Sarah waits until she's passed back through the double-hinged door to the kitchen before she responds.

"I was going to leave you."

"You still could," Dan offers.

She almost says, *Don't tempt me.* Instead she says, "Would that make you happy?"

"No."

"I think it would, in the long run." She adds, "I really was going to leave you."

"That's why you started driving again."

"I decided not to—and where do you get off, leaving and coming back?"

"Why did you decide to stay?"

"I couldn't write the break-up note. I'm a hack. Why did you decide to leave?"

"I was hungover and sad. I felt sorry for myself. I was only thinking about myself. I shouldn't've done it. I've been letting you down for a long time. I haven't been—"

"It doesn't matter. I forgive you."

The waitress breaks in: "Can I get either of you another beer? And, I don't want to rush you, but the check, will it be together or separate?"

"Together," Sarah says firmly. She does not look at the waitress.

"All right, I'll be right back." The waitress walks away.

"Okay, so which is it?" Dan asks.

"Which is what?"

"You said, 'It doesn't matter. I forgive you.'"

"Yeah?"

"Well, I don't think it can be both. I think it does matter—I've done you harm."

"I don't know what you want from me."

"I just want to talk."

"This isn't talking?"

He says nothing. She has defeated him. Why did she want to defeat him?

"I'm sorry," she says.

"I forgive you."

"Oh for god's sake, it's that faux-earnest bullshit that drives me crazy."

"I'm sorry."

"And there you go again."

The waitress returns with the check. Sarah passes her a credit card and with her arm accidently knocks over her beer.

"Goddammit." Dan frowns for a moment as the beer curls over the lip of the table. Then he starts reaching for napkins. The waitress, card in hand, disappears.

"So what do you want, Sarah?" he says as he mops up the spill.

"I don't know what I want. I don't want anything."

"You want to be left alone."

"Yes. No. I didn't say that. What do you want?"

"I want to say I'm sorry."

"You already did."

The waitress returns with the receipt. "You all can leave the mess for the busboy. He'll take care of it. Have a good evening."

Sarah signs the slip and stands up. "What now?"

"Maybe the Maulers are playing tonight."

He must have noticed her glancing at the hockey game. On the screen now two players are wailing on each other, the one has his arm over the other's shoulder, has him by the jersey. They turn a small circle as they jab each other in the stomach, punching at each other's faces, missing, glancing, turning.

She says, "I want to go home."

They walk back past the bars and the shops, and again he is silent. No, not silent, he is being patient. *I should stab him.* She is glad when they enter the little tunnel beneath the railroad tracks, where the rumble of the cars reverberates off the ceiling and no words can exist. On the other side they walk past the happy gardeners and two golden retrievers in a yard and still he is silent, but when they get to the porch he stops.

He says, "Can I tell you what I was going to say earlier?"

"You seem determined to."

"Can I?" He means it.

"All right, sure. Go ahead."

"I was going to say I'm sorry, not just for leaving and all that, but for how I've behaved since Sam died. I wasn't there for you the way I should have been. I'm sorry I never—"

"Please stop." She digs through her purse for the keys. He keeps going.

He says, "I'm sorry I never forgave you for the accident. I should've done it a long time ago, and I'm sorry that I didn't. I wronged you."

She shoves the key into the lock. "You can stop now. Please stop."

"This matters." He hesitates. Then he touches her arm so she'll look at him, and he says it: "I forgive you for the accident."

She looks away, wants to shout, opens the door, and like a fool she begins to cry.

She drops onto the couch like a woman in an old film, and when he sits beside her she hides her face in his shoulder. She cries for a long time, a loud gasping sort of sob, very ugly, and he holds her, even though she's worthless, the mom who killed her boy. He holds her and she sobs until she all she can do is shudder.

She wipes her nose on her sleeve. Outside the sun is setting. Shadows are stretching across the yard. The living room is growing dim.

She sits up, and he loosens his arms so she can stand. He follows her into the kitchen, which is already sunk in shadow, but neither of them reaches for the light switch. She wipes her nose again, then goes to the pantry. She pours two bowls of cereal and sits down across from him.

She says, "I hate the silence."

"Me too," he says, although she can see that he isn't quite sure. They've travelled out beyond his script. He says, "Maybe we should be noisy."

"What does that even mean?"

He doesn't know. He says nothing.

"I love you," he says.

"Is that enough?"

"I want it to be." He pauses. He speaks slowly and deliberately. He says, "Sam is gone and there's nothing we can do to change that, and I think we will always hurt, but I don't think that has to be the end of us."

"Dan, I have a duffle bag in the trunk. I really was going to leave you."

"You were too slow. I beat you to it."

"You chickened out. I wouldn't have. I would've been gone."

"I don't believe that."

"I guess we'll never know."

It takes a second for him to register what she's said. "You mean it?"

"I think I want to mean it." She looks down at her bowl. This is too much too fast. She changes her tone. "I can't leave, you'd fall apart. I mean, look at you, your shirt's on inside out."

"No it's not."

"It is. Your tag's sticking out."

He reaches around behind his neck. "Huh."

"Let's go to bed."

They leave the bowls on the table. In the bedroom she pulls off his shirt, chooses to do this, and gently eases him to the pillows. She rests her head on his bare shoulder, places a hand on his chest. He lays his hand on hers, and he does not push for more. He is following her lead, he is being patient—will he always be patient? When her eyelids sink shut she curls further into him.

Sleep, for her, comes quickly. He reaches for the lamp, then lies awake studying the shadows on the ceiling as he listens to her breathe. He falls briefly asleep and then wakes when she wakes.

It's still dark but she's sitting up, so he reaches for the lamp. His fingers are on the knob, but he hesitates. She is looking out the window.

"What's the matter?"

"Can't sleep."

"I'll sit up with you if you want."

"You don't have to."

"I know."

Light from the window rests on her cheek. She looks very beautiful and very sad. She says, "Sometimes I think it's Sam, but it's just the house settling."

He starts to say something but doesn't. Instead he rotates to sit next to her on the mattress. Out the window a thin light is catching on the ridges and roof-lines of the city. A trace of marigold rests on the mountains, a pre-dawn film coats the valley. The smoke holds the light as the train cars rumble in the distance.

Acknowledgements

Thanks, first and foremost, to my family for your boundless support, to the writing teachers who have shaped me and shown me the way, and to my many former classmates at Susquehanna University and the University of Montana who helped me find my voice.

Thank you to Summer Stewart and Unsolicited Press for helping bring this book into the world, and thank you to Kathryn Gerhardt for designing the book cover.

Thank you to Angela and Jess Correll, Bret Lott, and the Wedgwood Circle Institute for a generous grant that helped to support the writing of this book, and thank you to Nathaniel Lee Hansen and the rest of the staff at *The Windhover* for publishing a short story version of the opening pages of this book back in 2021.

And thanks to all the friends and family who have so generously read and responded to drafts of my work, both this piece and others. I hesitate to start naming you, because I know I'll be leaving out so many, but I have to mention Louie Land, Casey Oliver, Bruce and Alison Van Patter, and Anna, my wife, my best friend, my first and last reader.

Thanks also to my students past and present. Talking about writing with you all, especially your own writing, is something that helps me keep going. And thanks to all my colleagues at Messiah University, who are the most wonderful people to work with.

And finally, thank you, whoever you are, for reading these pages (yes, you!). No book is ever really finished until someone picks it up and brings it to life. Thank you for helping me finish mine.

About Ryan Rickrode

Ryan Rickrode is the author of *The Mountains May Depart* and *Accidents Will Happen: Essays & Photos.* He received his MFA in fiction and creative nonfiction from the University of Montana in 2013 and has been writing and teaching in Central Pennsylvania ever since. As a senior lecturer in English at Messiah University he teaches courses on creative writing, composition, and literature. As a writer he's interested in the ways narratives shape people, the ways in which faith and art can overlap, and the ways in which familiar stories like fairy tales can be made new once again. His shorter work has appeared in various places, including *Dappled Things, The Windhover,* and *The Cresset.*

You can read more of his work at ryan-rickrode.com.

About Unsolicited Press

Unsolicited Press is based out of Portland, Oregon and focuses on the works of the unsung and underrepresented. As a womxn–owned, all–volunteer small publisher that doesn't worry about profits as much as championing exceptional literature, we have the privilege of partnering with authors skirting the fringes of the lit world. We've worked with emerging and award–winning authors such as Sommer Schafer, Amy Shimshon–Santo, Brook Bhagat, Mari Matthias, and Amy Baskin. Learn more at unsolicitedpress.com. Find us on Twitter and Instagram at @UnsolicitedP.

www.ingramcontent.com/pod-product-compliance
Lightning Source LLC
LaVergne TN
LVHW040100080526
838202LV00045B/3715